THE … PER:
A L … HE
SCO … RDER

ROBERT SCOTT FITTIS

ZINCREAD

Published by
This edition copyright © 2024 by Zinc Read
Design and setting By Zinc Read
Email- zincread@gmail.com
ISBN-978-93-6196-269-1

CONTENTS

CHAPTER I.

O mirk, mirk is this midnight hour,
And loud the tempest's roar;
A waefu' wanderer seeks thy tower,
Lord Gregory, ope thy door.

—*Burns.*

IT was an early Spring eve in a year long before King James III. of Scotland perished in his flight from the lost field of Sauchieburn, and was succeeded on the throne by his son, Prince James, who headed the rebellion which resulted in the hapless monarch's assassination at Beaton's Mill.

On that Spring eve the setting sun, breaking through heavy cloud-masses, poured his red radiance athwart the snow-flecked summits of the hilly chain known as the Cheviots, the scene of Chevy Chase and of many another Border fight, and the boundary for a considerable distance between Scotland and the sister kingdom. The day had been dull and bleak, scarce enlivened by a transient glint of sunshine; nevertheless, the aspect of Nature somewhat indicated that the reign of "surly Winter" was over. As far as the eye could reach, the snow and ice had almost wholly melted from the face of the low country on either side of the hills; and the drooping snowdrop, emblem of purity, and harbinger of genial skies, decked the Frost-king's grave.

The red sun went down, leaving a trail of fire at the "gates of the west"; and a dreary quietude brooded on the hills—scant sign or sound of life being apparent save what the homeward-bound rooks made as they sailed, weary of wing, this way and that. But as the gloaming fell, a solitary pedestrian emerged from one of the passes on the Scottish side of the marches—a tall and stoutly-built but youthful man. A short cloak of untanned deerskin hung from his shoulders, being secured at the throat by a knot of thongs, and it partly hid a doublet, called, in Border phrase, a *jack*, of boiled leather, fitting close to the body, and strengthened on the breast (if not also all over the shoulders and sleeves) by small circular plates of hammered iron sewed on in overlapping fashion like the scales of a fish. A broad buff belt around his waist, held by a polished brass buckle, sustained an iron-hiked sword and a long knife or dagger, termed a *whinger*, hafted with buck-horn, curiously carved. His right hand—the other being studiously concealed under his mantle, and apparently carrying something rather bulky—was encased in a leathern gauntlet, the back of which was defended by little plates of mail like those on the jack. On his head he wore an iron bascinet cap, rusty and much dinted, and from under its rim straggled locks of dark brown hair inclining to curl. He had a thin, sallow, unprepossessing physiognomy, which expressed a combination of cunning and effrontery: two keen, grey eyes sparkled under heavy brows; and a slender moustache, lighter in colour than his locks, sparsely covered his upper lip; but the livid scar of a cicatrized wound, evidently from a sword-cut, adown his left cheek, gave, on close observation, a peculiar grimness to his otherwise sinister mien. Altogether, he might be considered as a typical Borderer of the time, rough-living, law-defying, rarely ever out of "sturt and strife."

On quitting the defile, he struck across a stretch of open moorland, over which the rising night-wind fitfully sighed among the furze. Now and then he paused and gazed eagerly behind, seeming to listen, as if dreading pursuit; but pursuers there seemed none, save the cloud-billows that rolled in endless succession over the dim hills and darkened above his head. The waste soon became both rugged and marshy, and a shallow rivulet, fed from the moss-hags, ran in a serpentine and perplexing course, necessitating its being repeatedly waded, but the water never came much above the traveller's ankles, and he wore a pair of strong buskins reaching to the calf of his leg. When he had finally left the sinuosities of the sluggish stream in his rear, he made a dead halt, as if come to the end of his journey, and scowled all around him in the gloom. Throwing back the left side of his cloak, he disclosed a young child, well wrapped up, and fast asleep, whom he was carrying, and whom he immediately laid down on the heath at his feet. The infant awoke, and began to whimper and wail. The man stood bending his moody gaze upon it till his eyeballs glowed with dusky fire.

"This nicht," he said, in a low tone, savouring of fierce exultation, "this nicht will the proud Southron grieve, and the bonnie lady greet in her bower, for the loss o' the young heir that was the hope o' their hearts. The retainers may scour hill and dale, and the pathless wilds echo the bay o' their sleuth-hound. Let them speed far and wide wi' horse and ban-dog. In my hand rests the young heir's fate. By the Black Rood o' Melrose! this is the revenge o' gentle Edie Johnston!"

He stamped on the ground, and could have crushed the infant under his heel; but he started back a pace, as if, indeed, the fiend of revenge had prompted such a thought in his troubled brain, and he revolted at it—but he revolted only for a moment, as the savage suggestion seemed to be followed by another equally remorseless. What did he now meditate? Was he one

Whom the vile blows and buffets of the world
Had so incens'd, that he was reckless what
He did, to spite the world?

Nervously his fingers clutched the hilt of his whinger, and he unsheathed it and waved it in the air, and then, stepping forward and stooping over the child, pointed the steel as if to deal a mortal stab. The weapon trembled in his grasp. Again the powers of compunction and shame overcame the murderous impulse. He raised himself erect, with an impatient ejaculation, and his armed hand fell slowly, and as if reluctantly, by his side.

"Frae sunset to sunset has this hand been feckless as a withered rush," he said. "In darkness as in licht I ha'e been weak as water. I micht ha'e flung the brat, like a stane, frae the brow o' a fathomless precipice, never mair to be seen but by the ravens: or he micht ha'e been thrown into a rushing stream that would ha'e swirled him awa' to the sea; and nae mortal could ha'e fyled me wi' the deed; and yet he is spared, as if his life were charmed by a spell o' power. Maun I, a gentle Johnstone, forget my wrangs? My faither fell in an inroad o' the Southrons: my mither was twice harried out o' her cot-house in the cleugh: and I—" He paused, and stroking his scarred cheek, glanced alternately around him and at the sobbing boy on the cold turf: then sheathed his whinger, lifted the babe, and strode hurriedly on his way.

Soon he came to a spring-well, a round, brimful *well-e'e*, fringed with furze. There he stopped, mused some space, and muttering a curse, suspended the child over the water, as if intending to let it drop and drown. But as he gazed fixedly on the limpid element, which shimmered under the dim sky, a lustrous planet shone out through the clouds and glittered in the natural mirror, the golden similitude sparkling up like the eye of an accusing spirit. It was what guilt could not withstand. The mystic gleam of the shadowy star smote the gentle Johnston to the soul. Drawing a harsh breath, he succumbed once more to a power that shamed his fierce nature. Huddling the infant under his rude mantle, he hurried from a spot where temptation had pressed him so strongly.

Straight northwards he held his route, with the shades of night deepening on what seemed a desert, where no living things seemed near save the heath-birds that started at his approach, and sped away with shrill screams. Some heavy drops of rain, "like the first of a thunder-shower," pattered on his head-piece and deerskin garment, and louder grew the sough of the gale, which prognostications of an inclement night caused him to quicken his pace. The child had now wept itself to sleep, and its bearer showed every care to screen it from the rough weather. Happily, the threatened storm blew by. But although the night settled down, the Borderer still travelled comparatively fast, with long, unwearied stride, as being well inured to exertion and well acquainted with the country which he was traversing. Indeed, we may not err in supposing that in the latter respect he could rival "stout Deloraine," of whom the Last Minstrel tells us that—

Through Solway sands, through Tarras moss,
Blindfold he knew the paths to cross;

* * *

In Eske, or Liddel, fords were none,
But he would ride them, one by one;
Alike to him was time or tide,
December's snow, or July's pride;
Alike to him was tide or time,
Moonless midnight, or matin prime.

Sometimes the traveller changed his course to a certain extent, inclining now to the right, now to the left, probably to avoid the neighbourhood of hamlets: his darkling journey was one of hours; but eventually the blustering blast swept away the clouds, and a frosty starlight shone down, enabling him to perceive that he was nearing the spurs of a range of low hills. On he went towards a wide ravine, and entering it, was soon plodding sturdily along a well-beaten but winding path, whilst the gale whistled shrilly through the underwood that clad both sides of the glen. As he progressed, his eye caught the feeble glimmer of a light in the distance, which he knew was not the twinkle of a star, and which was inconstantly seen and lost according to the turnings of the road.

"The auld keep o' Hawksglen at last!" he muttered. "An' gude fortune speed me, the seeds o' a double revenge will be sawn."

The glen debouched on what dimly appeared to be a spacious amphitheatre among the low hills, and in the foreground loomed the dark and turreted mass of a Border keep or castle, in a high casement of which burned the light that had been attracting the wayfarer's attention. He trudged forward to the strength, and speedily reached the outer wall surrounding it, which was machicolated or embrasured along the top for the discharge of all sorts of missiles on the heads of assailants attempting escalade: and now the angry, deep-mouthed bark of a dog within the wall broke the silence. The Borderer halted in front of an arched and strong portal, which was closed by a gate which he felt was faced with iron. He gave a peculiar whistle and then a halloo, which the dog answered vigorously, rousing others of its kind in their kennel in the rear of the place. But next the gruff voice of an elderly man responded to the Borderer's call from over the gateway—"Who goes there?"

The keen starlight could enable only the mere outline of the stranger's figure to be discerned. "A friend to Hawksglen," he answered.

"From whence, and on what errand?"

"From Rowanstane, and on matter o' life and death. I bring a letter to the worthy Elliot. Open the *vizzy*, and I will wait his pleasure."

"So, so: and bring you also the Rowanstane password?" demanded the scrupulous warder.

"Hand and glove."

Prompt was the result of this response—almost like the effect of the "Open, Sesame" of the Forty Thieves. The warder, confident that the knowledge of the password was confined to friends (and it was changed at intervals), descended from his coign of vantage; and after some preliminary clank of chains, an aperture, measuring scarcely a foot square, opened in the side of the portal, without the iron-sheeted gate, and about breast-high from the ground, whilst the dog was heard sniffing and growling along the bottom of the gate.

"Hand in your letter," said the warder.

The gentle Johnston deftly thrust the sleeping infant through the opening, and feeling that it was grasped by the other, turned without a word, took to his heels, and was lost in the gloom.

Judge of the amazement which seized upon the guardian of the portal when he found that instead of a letter he had received a bundle containing a young child, who being roughly awakened began to cry. For a moment was the warder struck speechless, but then, recovering his voice, he shouted through the aperture—"Hillo! man—what is this? Where's the letter? A bairn! what does this mean? Curse the knave! and he had the password too. A vile trickster! Down, Ranger! down, lad!"—for the dog was climbing upon him, and smelling at the child in his arms. "By our lady! a rare gift at midnight! What will Sir James say to it?

or his mother, either? I was a dolt to open the vizzy-hole; but the false-tongued knave swore it was a matter of life and death. The foul-fiend rive him! What ho! within there! Robin, Robin—up, man!"

A young serving-man rushed out to the gateway, with a spear in one hand, and a round buckler on his arm, and ejaculated—"What's the steer, Allan? I was dovering ower the ha' fire, after dipping ower deep in the ale-jack, and I thocht I heard the dogs bark."

"Bring a torch," cried Allan, "mayhap the wean is but a fairy changeling, and I must see to that ere it comes under our roof."

"The wean? whatna wean?" inquired Robin, rubbing his sleepy eyes with the knuckles of the hand that held the spear.

"You hear the wean yaumering: and fairy weans are ever girning—devil take them!"

"Allan, Allan, dinna speak o' *them* in sic a way, and at sic an hour. Ha'e you forgotten the auld rhyme?

"Gin you ca' me Imp or Elf,
I rede you look weel to yourself.
Gin you ca' me Fairy,
I'll work you muckle tarrie.

"I beseech you, Allan, bethink yoursel' that this is just the time when the *gude neighbours* are busiest for gude and ill."

"Pshaw!" exclaimed the warder. "I think a bad neighbour has been here. Fetch a torch, in Mahound's name!"

Robin hurried back to the hall, and, transferring his spear to his left hand that the right might be free, kindled a flambeau at the fire, and returned with it to the courtyard. The infant, on seeing the light, ceased crying, and stretched out his little hands towards the bickering flame.

"By the mass! a bonnie babe, and no fairy changeling, I'll be sworn," said Allan, and he shut the espial opening. "Let us now within doors."

They accordingly withdrew into the hall, where Allan sat down on a buffet stool at the side of the hearth, with the young stranger on his knee, while the watch-dog stretched itself at his feet, and the clamour of its companions in the kennel died away. Robin fixed his torch into an iron sconce projecting half a foot from the wall, stirred the faggots on the andirons to a blaze, and was then told the story of the adventure.

Seemingly nobody else in the place had been aroused, all remaining quiet; but Allan now directed his subordinate to call up one of the female domestics, to whose care the foundling should be committed till morning. The woman, when she came, being dubious as to whether the boy was not a fairy changeling after all, suggested the test usually applied to such supernatural impostors, namely, by "putting it on the fire to see if it wadna flee up the lum wi' an eldritch lauch!" But Allan was opposed to the experiment. The child's clothes were of fine materials, and around its neck was a slender gold chain of curious links suspending an antique golden reliquary; but there was no inscription on the trinket, or mark about the dress, to afford a clue to the little wearer's parentage.

The foundling being provided for, old Allan pulled his deerskin mantle closer around him, and went out to satisfy himself that the fastening of the aperture in the portal was secure.

"By our lady," he muttered, "I'll not open that vizzy again until daylight, although a score of stories of life and death should be told me. A small family might be foisted upon me ere morning."

CHAPTER II.

He's married a may, and he's fessen her hame;
But she was a grim and a laidly dame.
When into the castle court drave she,
The seven bairns stood wi' the tear in their e'e.
Nor ale nor mead to the bairnies she gave,
"But hunger and hate frae me ye's have."

—*Danish Ballad.*

TWENTY years elapsed after the midnight when the infant boy was left at Hawksglen Castle by the gentle Johnston, whom we dub with that epithet in accordance with the Border usage of characterizing the principal families, or clans, as the *haughty* Homes, the *bauld* Rutherfords, the *sturdy* Armstrongs, the *gentle* Johnstons, *et sic de cæteris*. But "gentle," as applied to the Johnstons, was an ironical misnomer, they being a peculiarly rude and turbulent race, living in "sturt and strife." A story is told that a Baron, who was at deadly feud with them, having captured several, ordered their heads to be cut off and flung into a sack, which he gave to one of his retainers to carry home; and the man, when he got the grisly burden upon his back, gave it a good shake, saying jocosely, "Gree amang yoursells, Johnstons!" Our Johnston seemed a full-fledged scion of this law-defying race.

Let us now fill up the gap of those twenty years with a brief recital of events which concern our tale.

Sir James Elliot of Hawksglen was the lineal descendant of a famous Border house; and a worthier representative of a baronial stock it would have been rather difficult to single out among his compeers. High renown had been earned by his ancestors in the feuds and wars of the marches. His father received his death-wound in resisting a Southron inroad some few years anterior to the period when our legend opens. Sir James, an only son and only child, was thus left master of wide domains when he had just passed his majority. His mother was an amiable lady; but after the loss of her husband she never regained that happy buoyancy of mind which had distinguished her during her wedded life. To all her dependants she was a kind and indulgent mistress, ever ready to forgive shortcomings, and to relieve the wants of humble vassals when overtaken by pinching poverty. Seeing that her son inherited the martial spirit of his sire, it became her aim to induce him to bury animosities and feuds, and to cultivate, as much as he could, and as far as the circumstances of the times allowed, the arts of peace. She meant well. But Sir James would say to himself, as he paced through his hall, and gazed on several grim portraits of the Elliots of Hawksglen with which it was decorated:—

"My mother's mild precepts would avail in some other age and land; but they are vain in this Border country, where every man rights himself by his own hand, and wins honour and esteem by martial valour. When every man draws his blade in his own quarrel, dare I keep mine unsheathed without incurring disdain and disgrace? Nay—in these times I must uphold the dignity of our house with the steel in my grasp and the corselet on my breast."

Sir James was ardent and fiery by nature, yet evincing generous and chivalrous impulses. In stature he rather exceeded the middle height, and had a manly and well-formed figure. His face was oval and swarthy-complexioned, its expression being mild and thoughtful in repose, but under excitement becoming instinct with strong animation. As yet in early manhood, he was unmarried, and so far as appeared had never been wounded by a shaft from Cupid's bow.

The midnight adventure at the gate exceedingly amazed the knight and his mother, and probably induced a certain suspicion in the latter's mind; but they resolved to shelter and provide for the child until its parents should be discovered. Every means were used to penetrate the mystery; but, owing to troubles which broke out along the Border, all inquiries proved fruitless, and even rumour was dumb. The child's habiliments and the ornament about its neck betokened that its lineage was above the common. Thus weeks and months sped away, and the foundling was treated with as much care and kindness as could have been bestowed upon a son of the family; which, indeed, the retainers could not help suspecting that he was, and therefore, they gradually refrained from rehearsing to others the story of his exposure at the gate.

The boy was healthy, with pleasing features, a soft skin, and a clear complexion. He soon became familiar with his new guardians; and the lady forgot her sorrows in ministering to his wants, and fondling him upon her knee. A priest from a neighbouring chapel admitted the foundling within the pale of the visible Church by the Sacrament of Baptism, and christened him by the name of Eustace, in memory of the lady's only brother who had died in infancy.

When Eustace had seen about a couple of years under the hospitable roof of Hawksglen, the lady was seized with a malignant distemper, which was destined to close her days. Despite the skill of physicians, the rapid progress of the disease could not be arrested: the lamp of hope burned dim: and now—

The mildest herald by our fate allotted
Beckoned, and with inverted torch did stand
To lead her with a gentle hand
Into the land of the great Departed,
Into the Silent Land.

As the lady was sinking, fully resigned to depart, she desired that the orphan boy should be brought into her presence, which was immediately done. Long ere this time she had become entirely persuaded in her own mind that he was really and truly of stranger blood. Raising herself with a last effort, she took him in her arms, and kissed his lips fervently; then turned to Sir James and said:—

"Son, I have one request to make ere I yield my fleeting breath. I have endeavoured to fill the place of the unknown mother of this fair child. In my last hour I leave him to your protection. I beseech you to befriend him until, by the workings of Providence, he be restored to the arms of his parents, or of his kinsfolk, which I am persuaded will some day take place. But until that day never let him feel that, under your roof, he is a stranger. In time you will lead a bride to the altar, and bring her to Hawksglen: children of your own will grow up around your knees: but, O, my son, never neglect this boy, never count him as an alien, while he abides under your roof. As I have cherished him till now, do thou cherish him still. This is my dying request, which I trust will be fulfilled."

The knight gave his solemn promise, laying his hand on the crucifix which the attendant priest was holding up before the dying lady. The child instinctively clasped her neck, and whimpered some broken words. The parting moment drew nigh. The last offices of the Church were performed; and soon the lady, in the serenity of hallowed hope, passed through the dark tide of Jordan to the better land.

The knight of Hawksglen was overborne by his bereavement. Shutting himself within his castle, for a space, he seemed to have forsaken the changeful world beyond its walls. Time sped its course; and at length the torch of Love slowly scattered the clouds of unavailing sorrow. Not long after Sir James left his seclusion he was smitten by the charms of Anne Rutherford, the only daughter of a Border baron.

Younger than himself, she possessed the witcheries of an exquisite form and a lovely face. It was whispered, *sub rosa*, that with her personal graces was united a disposition proud, self-willed, and shrewish. But what daughter of Eve, however fair, could claim perfection? Elliot, becoming her lover, was naturally incredulous of the faults or failings with which rumour charged her. To his glamoured eyes she appeared as a blooming rose without a thorn. She favoured his impassioned addresses: she accepted his hand: and, about eighteen months after his mother's demise, Sir James brought a fair young bride to grace his hall.

For a season wedded life went pleasantly at Hawksglen—the cup of the happy pair, who seemed absorbed in a dream of love, betraying no bitter drop. But the time came when the dream was broken. The mask which the lady had worn was withdrawn, and her husband was undeceived. She now evinced an unequal temper, a degree of whim and caprice, and an obstinate desire to subject everything to her will, which eventually dissipated much of Elliot's matrimonial happiness. In vain did he strive to wean her back to her former self: and he mingled with the troubles of the Border to counteract the feeling of disappointment.

An evil hour for the foundling boy was that in which Dame Anne came to Hawksglen. She was duly informed of the mysterious manner in which the child had been left, and of the injunctions laid upon her husband by his dying mother, which he felt it his bounden duty to respect. The lady affected to acquiesce in his sentiments; but at heart she thought otherwise. Secretly jealous that the boy might prejudice her own children in their father's estimation, and perhaps ultimately receive some portion of the Hawksglen lands (suspicions which cannot be considered as wholly unnatural), she soon endeavoured, by various little arts, to diminish her husband's regard for the foundling. Her enmity strengthened when, in about a year after marriage, she gave birth to twin daughters. After that event, little Eustace became more and more the object of the mother's dislike, and Elliot, anxious to soothe her feelings, relaxed in his attentions to the boy.

Eustace grew up a handsome youth, of a high spirit but an urbane and generous nature, which endeared him to all the dependants of Hawksglen. Lady Elliot, seeing in him more and more the likely cause of future trouble and danger, never ceased plying her insidious arts against him. Every trivial mistake or fault of his she reported to her husband in such exaggerated shape as was possible: and it seemed her aim to lower Eustace from the position of an accepted member of the family to that of a mere dependant, who had no claim to higher consideration. As she had no more children, and the want of a son embittering her jealousy of the foundling, she frequently told her husband that unless he secretly wished to adopt Eustace altogether, to the injury of his daughters' interests, it was doing wrong to maintain him in a station to which he had not the shadow of right.

The lady's twin daughters, Eleanor and Catherine, were beautiful girls, lauded by all who saw them. Eleanor, however, surpassed her sister in charms of form and feature, and had a gentle, guileless, trustful heart; while Catherine, fickle, passionate, and overbearing, seemed to be endowed with all the worst qualities of her mother. It was not remarkable that a mutual sympathy and attachment arose betwixt Eleanor and Eustace, or that antipathy towards him gradually gained possession of Catherine's mind, and was not concealed. Up to a certain period, Eustace was led to consider himself an orphan relative of the family: the sisters were allowed to entertain the same idea; but it was never mentioned what was the relationship, or whence he came. The retainers were constrained to avoid alluding in any way to the fact of his having been left at the gate: and, indeed, they generally formed the belief that he was Elliot's own son, and would some day be openly acknowledged. But Eustace, as he grew, had anxious musings concerning his parentage and the strange reticence manifested by one and all around him on the subject. He could not help fancying gloomily that some dark secret was associated with his birth, and would in the end be disclosed to his dismay.

Eustace, brought up amid the warlike turmoils of the Border, was trained, like other youths, to the use of arms, and occasionally bore his part in the field as Elliot's squire. In one desperate fray his daring saved the knight from slaughter, a gallant achievement which gained him the latter's highest regard. This was as gall and wormwood to Dame Anne. In a fit of ungovernable spleen, she told her daughters that the young hero was nothing better than a nameless foundling who had been thrown upon the charity of Hawksglen. She entrusted them with this startling knowledge as with a profound secret, which they were not to disclose to any without her express permission, for fear of drawing down upon her and them their father's displeasure. Probably the lady hoped that the revelation to her daughters would destroy the attachment betwixt Eleanor and Eustace, which, if allowed to exist, might result in love. Inconsiderate woman! she had no idea that she was taking the very step to thwart her own purpose. Catherine acted upon her mother's counsels, in holding Eustace in undisguised indifference. But with

Eleanor it was otherwise. To tell her that Eustace was the son of misfortune, cast upon strangers in his helpless infancy, was but to give new life to the affection for him which had grown in her mind.

Until about the age of one-and-twenty Eustace continued ignorant of the all-important secret, although distressing suspicions had long haunted his thoughts. But as intimacy betwixt him and Eleanor seemed, in the watchful lady's eyes, to increase, she dared again to break her husband's injunction. One day, when Sir James was absent from Hawksglen attending a Warden's Court, Eustace chanced to give the lady some offence, and appeared to treat her rebuke lightly, in revenge for which she told him the secret, adding that his unknown parentage was doubtless base, and that his position in the Castle should be that of the humblest menial. He had long anticipated something like this: yet the final disclosure came upon him like a thunderbolt, and he felt himself humiliated in the dust. He saw that the current of his life must now inevitably turn into another channel, and that his days at Hawksglen were thenceforth numbered. The world was wide, and he would seek his fortune.

CHAPTER III.

Adieu! Lochmaben's gates sae fair,
The Langholm holm, where birks there be;
Adieu! my ladye, and only joy,
For, trust me, I may not stay with thee.

Lord Maxwell's Good-Night.

DEEPLY chagrined, deeply grieved was the knight of Hawksglen, when, on his return, he was told by Eustace of what the lady had disclosed. Sir James, who hitherto had habitually evaded the young man's enquiries in such a way as to leave him to suppose that he was of kin to the family in some degree, however remote, now endeavoured to soothe his lacerated feelings; but this was a vain effort, as the truth of the story could not be denied. The utmost the knight could do was to dissuade his protege from leaving the Castle in his first flush of shame and indignation. "A soft answer turneth away wrath," but no soft words could allay the misery that filled the foundling's bosom.

The ice being thoroughly broken, Lady Elliot, undeterred by her husband's regrets and remonstrances, persevered in her bitter antagonism to Eustace, though covertly, for the most part. She justified herself that what she did was of imperative necessity. To her husband she justified herself on the score that affection was growing betwixt Eustace and Eleanor, which, if not nipped in the bud, might in the end lead to the disgrace of the house of Hawksglen. The reader may easily imagine what result followed. "A constant dropping weareth away stone." The strong-willed and implacable lady won her purpose. Elliot wavered, and eventually seemed to yield to her incessant persuasives. Coolness and, occasionally, slight discords arose betwixt him and his protege, by whom the change could not be misunderstood, a change that pointed to ultimate separation.

Eustace felt in his inmost heart that now he loved Eleanor more tenderly than in the days of his ignorance. She was become the loadstar of his aching heart. On the other hand, such an attachment looked hopeless—nay, more, that it was very madness to be cherished by a stripling who knew no kindred, and had no fortune. He had resolved to quit Hawksglen; but still he lingered. It was his anxious desire that, before taking the final step, he should have an interview with his lady-love, to explain his motives and to bid her adieu. For a while the opportunity was denied him—trivial obstacles interposing (perhaps designed by the cunning of Lady Elliot) to baulk his wish, and causing him to tarry still for the fortunate moment.

On a bright May day, Eustace was returning alone from the hills and woods in the vicinity of Hawksglen, among which he had listlessly spent hours since the early morning. He had gone forth from the castle on foot—not to seek the chase, for he took neither his favourite hound, nor his steed Roland (named after the famous Paladin of Romance); and though he carried a hunting-spear, it was for defence in case of danger. His only object was to roam and meditate on his dark prospects amid the solitudes of nature, unseen by an evil eye. On his homeward way through the woodlands he reached a lake, near which, and surrounded by a clump of sepulchral yews, appeared the ruined chapel or hermitage, beneath which was the burial-vault of the Hawksglen family, where lay the ashes of his generous benefactress. The castle was within a short distance; but its turrets were not visible from the banks of the lake, being hidden by a wooded height.

The sunlight beamed on the sheet of water, the placidity of which was unbroken by the slightest ripple, save when a trout leaped at a fly and sank with a slight plash, or a waterfowl skimmed lightly across the lustrous surface. Yonder, half-hidden among tall, aquatic plants, a gaunt heron stalked stealthily in the bordering shallows, intent upon its prey. The sky was serenely blue, and the air profoundly still, as if Zephyrus slept in his cave of the west. This quiet, secluded scene of wood and water, which the fairy court may have frequented in the moonlight, awoke in the youth's mind reminiscences of happy days past and gone. Wearied with his wanderings, he sat down upon the trunk of an aged tree which a recent storm had overthrown, and gave free scope to musings which recalled the "light of other days"—the "sunshine of the heart." In the dreamy hush of the woodlands, whose fresh, green foliage marked the advent of summer, the inconstant carol of a bird fell sweetly on the ear.

Eustace spent some time sitting on the fallen tree, and then resumed his walk along the banks of the lake. In person he was of moderate stature, slenderly but handsomely made, with an aspect that wore the impress of a manly mind, whether his birth had been high or low. His complexion, originally fair, the sun had tinged to a somewhat swart hue; his eyes were hazel, but a physiognomist might have read in them indications of soul-depression, and thick brown locks escaped in profusion from beneath his velvet bonnet, mingling with the white plume that drooped on his left shoulder. He was dressed in a cloth jerkin of forest-green, fitting close to his body, and girt about his middle by a belt from which depended a short falchion, the hilt of which was chased with silver; and silver also was the mouthpiece of a small bugle which was suspended beneath his left arm by a steel chain around his neck. He carried a hunting spear, which, however, bore no trace of having drawn blood that day. In fine, he had all the exterior of a gallant squire, as was, indeed, the position he held in relation to the knight of Hawksglen.

Leisurely pursuing his homeward route, our squire had surmounted the woody height, when he suddenly perceived on the winding paths below him, but half-hidden among the trees, a lady descending the declivity. Evidently she heard his footsteps, for she turned and glanced back. It was Eleanor Elliot. She wore a dark robe, open in front, and showing a blue velvet kirtle (or gown), the breast of which was covered by a stomacher of the like cloth, richly embroidered with threads of silver; and on her head was a small hood of purple silk, which did not prevent dark glossy tresses from clustering about a neck of alabaster hue. Her brow was smooth and high, her eyes blue as the sunny vault above her, and her soft and winning features bespoke a gentle nature. When she discovered Eustace all her maidenly sensibilities glowed on her cheeks. Not the fairest of the fair creations of the Greek imagination could have surpassed the lady, who now bashfully advanced to meet the youth who had gained her esteem and love; yea, and had also awakened her keenest pity.

Quick throbbed the squire's heart, and his countenance reddened, as he met and, laying down his spear, greeted the mistress of his affections. She took his hand, and giving it a gentle pressure, said—"I have been uneasy by reason of your prolonged stay; for, as you took neither horse nor hound with you, I thought your absence would be brief."

"Perchance it would be well for Hawksglen were I to depart, never to return," answered Eustace, sadly, unable to refrain from giving full utterance to the thought that was uppermost in his heart.

Instantly the lady became pale. But she replied in a calm tone—"Bethink you that there are those in Hawksglen who wish you well, and would have you not to brood over trifles."

"They are momentous trifles, since trifles you call them," said Eustace. "They are such trifles as have debased me in my own eyes."

"It was my lady-mother's fault, in hasty anger," faltered Eleanor.

"I will impute no blame to either of your parents," responded Eustace. "Your lady-mother only spoke what, in justice to me, she should have spoken long ago. It was right and just that I should know the truth. Why should I be protected and pampered by those upon whom I have no claim by ties of relationship? No, no, Eleanor, I have not the shadow of title to share the name, the favour, and the honours of the house of Hawksglen."

"I cannot bear to hear you speak thus: it cuts me to the heart," sighed Eleanor, shedding tears, which seemed to increase her lover's distress.

"All this misery would have been spared me had I perished on that night when the unknown Borderer left me at your father's gate!" exclaimed he, passionately, and striking his hand on his brow. But, after a moment's pause, he added, in a subdued tone—"I must bow to inexorable fate: I must yield to the tide which I cannot stem. But O Eleanor! forbear these tears."

She was weeping silently, but seemed more lovely in her attitude and aspect of sorrow. "Will the future never bring a time when the cold tide of misfortune will cease to flow betwixt us?" she murmured. "Heaven forbid!" she added firmly. "And I beseech you to think that better days will come, and that we need not part. You know not what end your destiny may work out. Trust it will be a good end. Why should you rashly judge that it will be bad?"

"Think as I may, Eleanor, our parting must come," said Eustace. "If I am to retain respect in others' eyes, I must carve out my own fortune. Avenues are open to adventurous spirits. Scottish soldiers are gladly welcomed at the courts of France, Italy, and other foreign states. Be my future fate what it may, I shall meet it with a fearless heart: and should I fail to win success—why, let me fail and fall, and be remembered only as one on whom an evil destiny had set its seal."

Both were silent for a space. Sorrowful emotion had exhausted language. Eustace gazed vacantly towards the castle of Hawksglen, which was dimly seen through the trees. Eleanor raised her swimming eyes to his face, and his look met hers. Never, perhaps, till now, in this dark and troublous hour, had the fair girl felt how devotedly she loved him—how deep was her interest in his fate since she realised that he was about to launch forth upon that ocean whose depths bury many a blasted hope.

"Let us prepare to part," said Eustace, breaking the silence. "To contemplate speedy separation is the surest way to lessen its pain when the inevitable hour arrives."

"Speak not of parting, I implore you!" she ejaculated, whilst her tears dropped fast. "The word sounds like a knell."

In what better terms could the fair girl have avowed her affection? Eustace tenderly grasped her hand. "We are no longer kinsfolk," he said; "but the love I bear you can never die. I will cherish it in my heart of hearts, however fortune may frown or smile."

She gave a loud sob, and fell upon his breast. He clasped her in his trembling arms, and kissed her cheek. Hark! a murmur of voices—the rustle of brackens, the crash of branches, the tread of hurrying footsteps—and Sir James Elliot and his lady stood before the pair! Eleanor started from her lover's arms, and shrieking, would have sunk to the earth had not her father sustained her. She swooned in his embrace.

"Behold the proof of suspicions which you have scoffed at as often as I expressed them," cried Lady Elliot, looking livid with anger, and darting a fiery glance at her husband. "This base-born minion will bring disgrace upon your house and name, and yet you are deaf and blind."

"Youthful folly," answered the knight. "But it shall never bring dishonour upon me. Eustace, both you and my daughter sadly forget your stations!"

"Forget!" echoed the lady. "Must such insolence be borne at *his* hands?"

"No, it shall not," said the knight. "Eustace, I have protected you since your infancy; but the obligation was fully repaid when you saved my life in battle, and therefore we shall cry quits, and part."

"The passing hour shall part us," said Eustace, calmly.

Without a visible sign of agitation, he lifted his spear from where it lay among the brackens, and turning upon his path, plunged into the thicket and vanished from sight. The die was thrown: the old tie was snapped asunder; and he was a forlorn exile from the only home which he had ever known.

The world was all before him, where to choose
His place of rest, and Providence his guide.

He hastened through "woods and wilds," with no immediate purpose in view save that of quitting the domains of Hawksglen. On he went, heedless that the hours sped away on fleet wings. But he paused to consider his course when the sun was setting amid amber cloudlets, and the balmy influence of the "merry month of May" was in the gentle western breeze that now fanned the wanderer's hot cheek. He remembered a hamlet at some distance, where he thought of staying till next morning; and fortunately he carried a well-filled purse, which would answer all requirements for a time.

CHAPTER IV.

Wi' cauk and keel I'll win your bread,
And spindles and whorles for them wha need.
Whilk is a gentle trade indeed,
    To carry the Gaberlunzie on.

—*The Gaberlunzie-man.*

As the self-exiled Eustace pursued his route, in troubled reverie, he was soon hailed by a masculine voice from a straggling thicket near the wayside. Glancing in that direction, he saw a man issue from among the trees, and step towards him. The man was in the humble garb of a gaberlunzie, and seemed a fair representative of the trade of mendicancy, which was numerously followed throughout the country in that age, and for ages afterwards. At a little distance he looked rather youngish; but on nearer approach he was seen to be elderly, perhaps about his grand climacteric. He was tall, spare, and erect of figure, lithe of limb, and with a shrewd, honest, weather-beaten, but unwrinkled countenance, and short, iron-grey locks appearing from under his broad blue bonnet. A wallet was slung at his back, and a leathern pouch or purse at the side of his waist-belt, in which was stuck a sheathed whinger, and he carried a stout *kent* or long staff with an iron spike at the end, which would prove a formidable weapon when wielded in a fray by a strong hand. Eustace stopped, and was saluted by the stranger, who doffed his bonnet and bowed low. Understanding that the man's object was the solicitation of charity, Eustace gave him an alms which was received with effusive thanks, and dropped into the pouch.

"You'll be gaun the Greenholm way, master?" said the stranger, deferentially.

"I am. But no farther than the village for the night."

"Weel, master, I'm just gaun the same gate: and aiblins you winna be offended though a gaberlunzie should jog at your heels?"

Eustace looked at him, with a complacent smile, without replying to the question; but the smile seemed to be intended and accepted as a negative reply. They went on together, side by side.

"It's a braw and bonnie nicht," said the beggar, surveying the surrounding scenery with a gratified eye, and pointing here and there with his staff. "A braw May nicht indeed. Look to the lift—look to the earth—there's beauty owre a'. See—the parting beams o' the sun linger on the bald, rocky brow o' yon hill, like a crown o' glory, while a' the dell aneath is losing itsel' in the shadow, and the haze is rising that will soon ha'e the appearance o' a loch. You hear the sweet sangs o' the birds, the sough o' the westland wind, and the everlasting plash o' yon burnie that gushes owre its linn. The gowden clouds are sailing solemnly as if to strains o' angel-music. How pleasant to wander, free as air, amang Nature's charms!"

"It is so," said Eustace, surprised at the elevation of the beggar's tone. "But life passes through gloom and storm as well as through sunshine. We have our flowery May, and we have our wintry December. In some deep cleugh among the hills patches of last December's snow will still be lying."

"Ay, truly," returned the mendicant, glancing keenly at the youth. "And, if I may presume, you seem to me, frae your words, to ha'e borne the brunt o' a stormy fortune, though you're o' gentle rank, and in the morning o' life, and no a grey carle like me, wha has warsled wi' the warld sae lang an' sair."

"No one, whatsoever his station, is exempt from the frowns of fickle Fortune," said Eustace. "In sooth, the more exalted the station, the more exposed is it to adverse blasts."

"True, master, true," responded the gaberlunzie. "The whirlwind, or the levin'-bolt, that rives and scatters in flinders the sturdy oak o' a hunder years, spares the wee bush that grows lowly at its root."

"But how came you, who must have been a man of mettle in your prime, to take to this wandering life?" questioned Eustace. "The world must have gone ill with you."

"Ay, master, just as it has gane ill wi' mony a better man," answered the gaberlunzie, with a dry smile and a shrug of his shoulders. "I was born and bred in a peasant's cot in the Lothians, and mony a year I spent in the service o' my faither's Laird. But service, you ken, is nae inheritance: and I ne'er rase aboon the lot o' a simple hind, trauchling frae morning till nicht. I saw a' my kith and kin laid aneath the yird. Sae I flung the gaberlunzie-wallet ower my shouther, and here I am."

"And is the trade better to your liking and your profit?"

"Muckle better," replied the wanderer. "I stravaig the country at my ain will, and the calling thrives wi' me. I use my e'en and lugs, and aften see and hear what ithers dinna dream o'. A Border mosstrooper is aye richt glad to pay for my tidings, whilk may shew him how to mak' a stroke o' gude luck, or to save his neck frae the gallows. The same wi' a Border knicht or baron, wha may be threatened wi' the onfa o' an enemy. Again, if a fair dame, shut up in her faither's bower, has a love message to send to the lad o' her heart, wha sae able to carry it, whether by word o' mouth or in a sealed billet, as Willie Harthill, the gaberlunzie? I pass free frae the clay-bigging to the lordly ha', and am aye welcome. Sae, master, the trade thrives weel, and if the times were mair troubled, it micht thrive better—wha kens?"

The wayfarer soon came within sight of the hamlet of Greenholm, which lay nestled in a hollow among grassy hills, whose sides were dotted with sheep, which shepherds and their dogs were collecting to fold for the night.

Eustace was asking some question when Willie stopped him with—"Hush! master. We are coming to haunted ground. Do you see thae bourochs—thae bonnie green knowes, that are freshened by the sweetest dew and blessed by the silveriest moonshine at midnicht hours?"

"Haunted ground!" muttered Eustace, not without a faint feeling of awe. He saw on one side of the path several gentle knolls, covered with verdure, and environed by broom bushes like a hedge; and coming nearer he perceived on the knolls some of those gracefully-formed grassy circles which so long perplexed the ignorance, and confirmed the superstition, of bygone ages. Tracing those mystic rounds, the Fairies were believed to dance their gay galliards in the moonlight. Our travellers paused a moment to contemplate the scene of Elfin revelry.

"You'll ha'e whiles seen the *gude neighbours*, master?" said the gaberlunzie.

"Never," answered Eustace; "the fairies are but figments of the imagination."

"Dinna ca' them by that name, whatever you may think o' them," said the other hastily. "You may freely ca' them *gude neighbours*; but *seelie wichts* is the name they like best; for they say themsells—

"'Gin you ca' me *Imp* or *Elf*,
I rede you look weel to yourself:
Gin you ca' me *Fairy*,

I'll work you muckle tarrie:
Gin *Gude neighbour* you ca' me,
Then gude neighbour I will be:

But gin you ca' me *Seelie wicht*,
I'll be your friend baith day and nicht."

"My forbears ha'e seen them: and I saw them twice mysel' langsyne on the green at the burn-side ahint our laird's Grange. What mair proof wad you seek? And as to their rings on the grass, the auld rhyme says—na, we maun gang on a bit," he said, checking himself, "we maun get ayont the bourochs before I venture on a rhyme that ca's the seelie wichts by a wrang name."

They jogged on beyond the knolls, and then Willie, believing himself out of supernatural danger, recited the following words of warning—which, however, he did not presume to aver were the composition of some fairy versifier:—

"He wha gaes by the fairy ring,
Nae dule nor pine shall see;
And he wha cleans the fairy ring,
An easy death shall dee.
But he wha tills the fairies' green,
Nae luck again shall ha'e;
And he wha spills the fairies ring,
Betide him want and wae;
For weirdless days and weary nichts
Are his till his dying day."

Our travellers soon reached the outskirts of the village, which was situated at the foot of a hill, with a shallow stream running in front of the cottages, which all stood, in irregular order, on its farther bank. A few old and gnarled trees raised their leafy heads above the roofs. In the back-ground appeared a lofty square tower of the order known on the Border as *Peels* or *Peelhouses*, to which the neighbouring cottagers usually resorted for protection against an inroading enemy. The Peel had scarcely any windows save near the battlemented roof; but the walls were pierced with many shot-holes, and it was surrounded by a high and thick wall, with a strong portal. In the vicinity was a mound, on which stood a moss-monolith or stone-pillar, perhaps the last remnant of a Druidical circle, or perhaps the memorial of some doughty warrior who fell in battle ages before.

The hamlet looked poor and miserable, being composed of about a score of clay-walled and thatched cottages, which, on the occasion of an English inroad, would be unroofed and left empty, to let the foes work what ravage they might; but there being little or nothing to burn, the huts could be restored when the foray was over. The burn was bridged here and there by old planks, and stepping-stones were also seen in the water at different places. A troop of half-clad children romped about the burn-side; and some old men sate at doors, in the evening light, repairing rude implements of husbandry. When the two travellers were perceived by the youngsters, they eyed them attentively, and then, with a shrill outburst of delight, came running forward, and danced about the gaberlunzie, like the very elves of whom he had been speaking. He patted the heads of the girls, and chucked the chins of the boys, saying, meanwhile, to Eustace—"The bairns a' ken the gaberlunzie. But are you kent here?"

"I am a stranger to the place," answered Eustace.

Willie then addressed the merry group around him—"Enough o' daffing, bairns. Come awa' and let me get into ane o' your couthy hames; for I am sair wearied this nicht wi' lang travel."

The imps set up another shout, and proceeded to escort the twain to the village, where most of the cottagers were attracted to their doors by the clamour.

"Weel, master," said Willie, "will you condescend sae far as tae tak' pat-luck wi' me, or maun you ha'e a lodging for yoursel'?"

"One lodging will serve us both for the night," answered Eustace. "I am not proud, and I am glad of an honest companion. I neither know nor care whether the people here recognise me; but recognition would do me no harm. Meantime you can tell them, if required, that I had lost my way before meeting with you."

"And what name do you pass under?"

"Ruthven Somervil," returned Eustace, without hesitation, having previously decided on that adoption. The surname was an honourable one on the Border, and had been so since the legendary times when an early Somervil killed a serpent or dragon that kept its lair in a wild glen of Linton parish in Roxburghshire—as the old rhyme commemorates:

The wode Laird of Laristone
Slew the worm of Worm's Glen,
And wan all Linton parochine.

"But," added Eustace, "you need repeat the name to nobody."

The cottagers greeted the gaberlunzie with kindly welcome; and the dress of Eustace bespoke for him a respectful reception, no one seeming to know who or what he was. A grey-headed sire and his dame invited the travellers into their dwelling. Homely viands were set before them, of which they partook with relish—Eustace being served apart. When the meal was over, neighbours came in, and solicited Willie to sing them some of his stock of songs. He complied, and a full supply of nappy liquor being procured at Eustace's expense,

The nicht drave on wi' sangs an clatter,
And aye the ale was growing better.

When the jovial company broke up, the aged host showed Eustace into a closet, furnished with a couch, and then bade the gaberlunzie ascend by a trap-stair to the loft above, where he would find a sleeping place. Eustace stretched himself on his couch, and slumber speedily overtook him. He slept soundly until the morning sun, beaming on his face, awoke him from strange dreams.

CHAPTER V.

Now loud the heedful gate-ward cried—
"Prepare ye all for blows and blood!
Wat Tinlinn, from the Liddle-side,
Comes wading through the flood."

—*Lay of the Last Minstrel.*

WHEN our two road-companions left their pallets and returned to the kitchen or main-room of the cottage, the goodwife was setting out materials for breakfast. The windows were wide open, admitting the fresh breath of dewy morn to purify and sweeten the atmosphere that had pervaded the domicile during the night. Early as was the hour, the village was astir for the labours and duties of the new day, and the horn of the cowherd who was driving the "milky mothers" to the pastures—the singing of birds—the cawing of rooks—and the ceaseless babble of the burn—formed a medley of sounds right cheerful to hear. With fair appetite our wayfarers attacked the viands spread before them; but ere they had finished their repast a sudden clamouring of tongues and a trampling of horses made them pause and listen. Am I pursued? thought Eustace—or, as we shall now call him, Ruthven Somervil—and he and his companion rose, and going to a window, saw a band of armed troopers riding slowly through the village, their appearance causing a general commotion among its denizens. But at the first glance our hero satisfied himself that the strangers were not retainers of Hawksglen.

The better to observe the party, Harthill and the old host went out to the door, but Ruthven remained at the window. The horsemen were seven in number, jackmen or retainers of Laird or Baron. All wore strong leathern "jacks" or doublets; iron bascinet caps or round helmets with cheek plates, but no visors; and heavy jack boots with large spurs. They were armed, after the usual fashion, with spears, swords, and daggers—the spears being of the enormous length of nearly six ells, according to the regulation in the Act of the Scottish Parliament of 2nd April, 1481. The foremost rider, the apparent leader of the party, wore, in the front of his bascinet, a few sprigs of the golden broom, which Ruthven knew was the cognizance or badge of Gilbert Lauder, a grasping and restless laird, whose Peel was a number of miles distant.

"There maun be something in the wind," said the gaberlunzie to his host, "when gentle Edie Johnston is in the saddle sae early."

Edie Johnston? Yea, the leader was the very man who had left the child at Hawksglen gate! He looked much older now, older than perhaps he actually was. Twenty years and more of a habitual course of "sturt and strife" had done their work upon him: his complexion was darker, his form more spare, and the scar on his cheek, which he would carry to the grave with him, gave his countenance a settled and forbidding gloom. Ruthven gazed at him with surprise, for, though he could not remember having ever seen the man before, yet the face seemed one that had frequently haunted his dreams, and now the figment was embodied to his view.

Johnston, on coming up to the cottage, uttered an exclamation, and halting with his men, leaned aside, and tapped the gaberlunzie good-humouredly on the shoulder with his long lance, saying—"My worthy crony! Hard to tell where friends may meet. Troth, I ha'ena seen your blythesome face for near a twalmonth since yon nicht I fell foul o' you instead o' gleyed Hecky Lapstane, the Selkirk souter; but I hope you soon forgot the broil."

"My cloured pow wasna sae soon forgotten," answered Harthill. "But I bore you nae grudge, kenning that you ettled at the souter's croon and no at mine."

"Richt, Willie," replied the trooper. "When the drink's in, the wit's out—a saying as true as Gospel. But I was sair vexed next day when I cam' to my sober senses, and minded o' what betell."

"It was weel for you," cried a village youth, on the other bank of the burn, who was hacking wood; "it was weel for you that you had to do wi' souters and gaberlunzies, else you michtna seen the neist day."

"Hooly, hooly, Dandie," whispered a companion in the speaker's ear. "Dinna raise his ill bluid. Let sleeping dogs lie."

"Hooly yoursel'," returned the youth. "If a' tales be true, he has done ill to my kin, as weel as to fremit folk no far awa'. He canna deny—and though he denies wha cares?—he whiles sell'd himsel' to our auld enemies ower the Border, and harried Scots land for them."

"Ralph Kerr's nowte were driven last Martinmas," said another voice. "Wha did that?"

"And Widow Janfarrie's hoggs the Michaelmas before," added a third.

It was evident that the gentle Johnston was in bad repute among some, at least, of the Greenholm folks; and he was constrained to notice their aspersions.

"What?" he ejaculated, with a sardonic grin, which showed that he had lost some of his front teeth. "Are a' the misdeeds on the Border to be laid to my charge?"

"Your hand has been in a hantle o' them," retorted a fourth voice.

Edie's eyes glowed with dusky fire, and shaking his spear, he said—"If another foul word be spoken against me, by the mass! but I'll gi'e some o' ye bluidy croons for your pains. Let the man that I ha'e wranged stand forward, and I'll answer him. If it werena that him I serve and your ain Laird are hand and glove, I wad tak' amends for what has passed already."

The mention of their own superior had a good effect upon the traducers; for, one by one, they slunk away, muttering to themselves what they did not venture to speak aloud.

"Cowardly tykes!" said Edie. "Weel did I ken that a word frae my lips wad be worth mair than anither man's blow."

The gaberlunzie now stepped out from the doorway, and patted the neck of Johnston's nag, saying—"You wear Ballinshaw's favour in your cap again. I thocht that when you left his service, on a quarrel, it was for gude an' a'."

"Sae I thocht, and sae I said," answered Johnston. "But the Laird soon found out that he couldna want me; for I had been to him as his richt hand. He sent for me and southered up matters, and I put the bonnie broom in my cap again."

"And what's your errand this morning, if ane may daur to speir?"

"A peacefu' errand," responded Edie. "Ballinshaw and Royston Scott o' Altoncroft ha'e differed anent the marches o' their lands. In my judgment, a wheen spear-thrusts and sword-slashes wad ha'e decided the dispute speedily and honourably, according to Border use and wont, and I ga'e Ballinshaw my mind to that effect. But, by ill luck, Sir Robert Home, the Shirra, got inkling o' the affair, and sent word to baith Lairds that if they broke the peace, he wad visit them baith wi' the King's vengeance. On the ither hand, he advised them to appoint him as arbiter atwixt them, and he wad decide justly on the plea."

"He's a worthy man Sir Robert," said Willie. "Ever since he cam' into power in this shire, he has done his best to mak' the law respected."

"Law respected! whew!" exclaimed Edie, with a scoffing whistle. "Baith Lairds swithered about coming to blows, and agreed to mak' the

Shirra their arbiter, and to gi'e leal and true obedience to his award. They are to meet him on the disputed ground this day at noon-tide: and I ha'e been gaun the rounds, warning men that can mak' aith in Ballinshaw's favour to attend at the place and hour appointed, and bear soothfast testimony, as I am to do mysel'. Will you gang ower the way? I'll be glad to toom a tankard wi' you after the sport."

"Whaur's the ground?"

"The meeting is to be at the Deadman's Holm—ten lang mile awa."

"I ken the place weel," said the gaberlunzie, "and I'm a-mind to gang, just as I gang to a' gatherings whaur there's chance o' bountith and gude cheer."

"See that you keep tryst, Willie," responded the gentle Johnston. "Now lads," he cried, "the day is advancing, and we maun mak' speed. We ha'e mair witnesses to warn."

Instantly he and his band shook their bridles, spurred their horses, and clattered at the gallop through the village. The gaberlunzie came in from the door, and he and Ruthven proceeded to finish their morning meal.

"Yon's a dare-deevil." said Willie. "He wad as soon drive cauld, cauld steel through a man's brisket as I cut up this black pudding": and then, in answer to Ruthven's anxious enquiry, the wanderer related what he knew of the gentle Johnston's history: "Edie canna be muckle blamed; for, like mony anither Border lad, he was brocht up to rough living frae his young years—his faither being a famous reiver and lifter till he met his death in a fray with the Warden's men. Edie was but a stripling when he was cuisten upon the world. For some time he lived by his ain hand, like his forbears, but syne took service as a common jackman, whiles on this side o' the Border, whiles on the ither—Edie caring only for the side that brocht him the best pay. Mair nor ance he has rubbit shouthers wi' the gallows, whilk, I fear, will be his end."

The gaberlunzie then began to suggest that our adventurer might accompany him to the Deadman's Holm to witness the proceedings of the arbitration. After some dubiety, the youth, who had decided as yet on no special destination, gave his consent, but deemed it absolutely necessary that, in going to the meeting, he should adopt a disguise to baffle recognition, and accordingly he requested his host to procure a humble garb for him. What he wanted was obtained for a small sum of money, and he donned a common dress, which was likely to suit his purpose. Retaining only his sword and dagger, he left his cast attire, with his hunting horn and spear, to be kept by the old villager until reclaimed.

Everything being satisfactorily arranged, Ruthven and the wanderer bade good-day to their host, who, being liberally rewarded for his hospitality, stuffed Willie's wallet with what victuals would suffice for the day; and the strangely-assorted companions set forth.

The day was beautiful, the welkin pure as the brow of childhood, and the earth robed in all the flowery freshness of the merry month of May. The heart of the exile was lightened of its brooding despondency by the sweet influences of Nature, and seemed to beat in unison with the summer joy. But the relief was transient. Gloomy thoughts returned, like dark clouds over a sunny sky, imparting a sadness to his countenance, which, his fellow-traveller observing, he sought to divert his mind by singing legendary ballads, and telling tales of haunted ruins, fairies, and general diablerie—all which, if failing in their true object, served to beguile the tedium of the way.

Travelling leisurely, our wayfarers, in a few hours, approached the scene of the judicial meeting. A company of troopers and footmen, with the Sheriff at their head, marched past, showing that the appointed hour was drawing nigh. Our travellers, on reaching a sparse wood, halted in the cool shade, and partook of refreshments from the gaberlunzie's wallet, which, being well stored, furnished a "feast of good things," and their drink was supplied by a slender streamlet that flowed murmuring among the trees, and sparkling in the broken sunbeams that glinted through the foliage overhead. After satisfying their appetite, they pursued their route, and, having ascended an eminence, descried a dark tower with turrets in the distance, which the gaberlunzie said was the Keep of Ballinshaw, near which stretched a wide expanse of level moorland, yellow with the broom and whin.

They quickened their pace, and soon heard an occasional winding of horns and the loud voices of men, which directed their steps to a broad hollow, or holm, on the verge of the moor farthest from the tower of Ballinshaw, and traversed by a burn, the banks of which were lined with aged saughs. There a considerable concourse of men had assembled, partly armed, retainers and partly peasantry, straggled about on both sides of the water, some of the former trotting up and down on horseback, some lounging on the grass casting dice, whilst their steeds grazed at random. In the midst of a well-appointed band of jackmen appeared a knight in half-armour, Sir Robert Home, the Sheriff, a man of middle age, with a grey beard. A young page attended him, bearing aloft a spear with a gauntlet or glove on the point of it, as the well-known border emblem of peace and amity. Behind their superior stood the footmen of the party, some six Sheriff Officers or "Serjeants," as they are distinctively termed in the old Acts of the Scottish Parliament. Their status was denoted by *white wands* in their hands; *blazons*, or medallions of brass, charged with the royal arms, displayed upon their breasts; and *horns* (for denouncing rebels) hanging from their necks by iron chains; while, for greater security in those troublous times, when law was so often defied, each officer was armed with a sword, and wore an iron bascinet cap, and gloves of mail.

CHAPTER VI.

The times are wild; contention, like a horse
Full of high feeding, madly hath broke loose,
And bears down all before him.

King Henry IV., Part Second.

NEITHER of the contending parties had yet appeared on the ground, although the hour of meeting was rather past, as shown by the position of the sun in the cloudless firmament. The Sheriff was indicating signs of uneasiness at the delay. But now, on the farther confines of the broomy moor, a dark, moving object was descried, which soon resolved itself into a rider, and by and by into a monk, habited in black frock and cowl, and mounted on a mule, which was trotting at an easy pace. This was an ecclesiastic, who had been summoned from the nearest religious house to assist in administering the judicial oath to the witnesses at the arbitration. The breast of his frock was bulged out by what had the appearance of a volume within it, which was retained in its place by the cord encircling his waist. It was a frequent custom of the time that priests went about the country, when required, to perform the sacraments of matrimony and baptism, carrying their missal in their breasts, and thereby acquiring the vulgar appellation of *book-a-bosoms*. Thus, we are told, in the *Lay of the Last Minstrel*, about the goblin page, when he discovered the magic book which William of Deloraine carried, that

Much he marvell'd a knight of pride
Like a book-bosom'd priest should ride.

The monk's mule bore the commonest caparisons, but several small bells hanging at the bridle-reins, so that we may say of the rider, what old Dan Chaucer said of his pilgrim-father on the merry journey to Canterbury shrine, that

When he rode, men might his bridle hear
Gingling, in a whistling wind, as clear
And eke as loud as doth the chapel bell.

The dark brother rode up to the Sheriff, who, with a courteous salute, desired him to take position by his side.

Ere much longer time had fled a company of horsemen arrived—Lauder of Ballinshaw and retainers, prominent among which last was the gentle Johnston. Such of the party as were intended for witness-bearing dismounted. Ballinshaw was a wiry, short-statured man, bearing his advanced years well; but his sallow and shrivelled visage had an air of avarice and duplicity, which was attempted to be hidden under an evident mask of careless candour. Offering his hand to the Sheriff, he delivered himself as follows, in a wheezing, jog-trot tone:—

"My humble service, Sir Robert, to uttermost power. I'm a wee ahint the appointed time; but some o' my witnesses were slack in coming forward; though I'm glad and proud to think that you'll find them a' leal and true men that wadna forswear themsel's for a King's ransom. Gude kens! I dinna wish to wheedle ony man oot o' his richts, far less my neighbour, Royston Scott, though he has lang borne enmity to me without cause. I see I'm before-hand wi' him: he's no' on the field yet."

"No," answered the Sheriff, "and if he delays much longer, I shall adjourn the meeting to another day."

"He's a thrawart tyke, as I ken to my cost," replied Ballinshaw, shaking his head. "We micht ha'e lived in gude neighbourhood, and settled a' disputes ower a friendly flagon; but na—he wad carry a'thing ower my head, kenning that I was a man o' peace. I durstna hunt ower the ground ayont the burn. He slauchtered my hounds, chased my serving-men, and vowed that if I mysel' daured to set foot across the holm, he wad be my death. Now, he ne'er had a shadow o' richt to the ground; for, time out o' mind, my forbears hunted ower it to the foot o' the hill yonder, without let or hindrance."

"And I presume you are possessed of legal evidence to prove your claim?" said the Sheriff. "Charters, and so forth?"

"Deil a scrap o' write ha'e I, my lord—mair's the pity," responded Lauder, feigning a smile. "Ance in a day there was a muckle iron-banded kist, panged fu' o' musty parchments, that stood in the closet o' the south turret; but a'e nicht the closet took fire, and kist and charters were burned to eizels, and gaed up in the air like peelings o' ingans. Still, my witnesses are passing gude; and, Sir Robert, let me say—"

"They shall be heard in due course," said the Sheriff. "Defer your statements till the proper time. I cannot listen to either party until both are present."

"That's gude law; for ilka man's tale is gude till anither's be tauld," returned Ballinshaw. "But what I ha'e yet to say is meant for your private ear."

"My duty is to act publicly, not privately," said the Sheriff; but not willing to be harsh, he added—"If what you wish to say does not concern the case in hand, I am ready to hear you. Say on, and be brief."

Ballinshaw took hold of the knight's bridle, and led him slowly away out of earshot of the assemblage. "Sir Robert," said the crafty Laird, coming to a stand, and speaking low, "as you cannot but be satisfied in your ain mind that I am likeliest, frae auld use and wont, to ha'e the richtfu' claim to the disputed ground—"

"Stay," interrupted the Sheriff, angrily. "This still affects the arbitration. Would you have me to prejudge the case? I cannot, in conscience, listen to you."

"A moment, Sir Robert, a moment," implored Lauder, holding tightly by the bridle. "I was thinking that, as you will mind, when we were baith in our youthy days—though I had the advantage o' you in years—how you whiles cam' to Ballinshaw wi' your faither; and how I took you amang the bosky knowes to gather brambles and blaeberries; and sometimes made a fishingwand and tackle for you, and sorted your bow and arrows, and helpit you to climb trees for nests—ah! thae were lichtsome days: now, I say, I was thinking that maybe for langsyne and its friendship, you could ca' me through the present troublesome business wi' little din—and I wad mak' up a purse—"

"Hah! you would pollute the source of justice by a foul bribe?" ejaculated the Sheriff, frowning deeply.

"Siller can do nae man harm," said Lauder, with an insinuating smile. "You ken the proverb—'There's a time to gley, and a time to look even': and wherefore shouldna a man gley for the sake o' his ain pouch? Far be it frae my wish to wrang ony man; but Royston Scott has lang been kent as ane that cares na a whistle on his thumb for a' the laws and shirras in braid Scotland; and it wadna be amiss in you, Sir Robert, to gi'e an auld friend a feather out o' sic a corbie's wing. I hear you're pressed by Ben Magog, the Jew of Berwick, for some siller he lent you on bond. Settle this business in my favour, and I'll help to clear you o' the Jew's grip."

The Sheriff, in silent scorn, released his rein from Lauder's hold. At that moment, the blast of a horn pealed from the adjacent hill, and a cry arose—"Yonder is Altoncroft at last, wi' a sturdy clump o' spears at his back!" The Sheriff, avoiding Lauder's renewed clutch at his bridle, rode back to his train.

The summit of the height was crowned by a troop of horsemen, whose arms and armour flashed in the sunlight. They numbered double Ballinshaw's party, which fact caused him to look nervous, and to whisper, in an agitated voice, to the gentle Johnston, who, with a stout aspect, strove to reassure him. The approaching band spurred hard down the grassy slope of the hill, and traversing the low ground like the shadow of a flying cloud, soon reached the rendezvous and drew bridle. Altoncroft was a man in the vigour of life, and of a tall and muscular figure, with a harsh cast of features, and fierce grey eyes. He wore a leathern jack, plated with mail on the breast and the sleeves, and a steel cap, from which a long red plume drooped down his back, whilst his weapons were lance, sword, and dagger.

"You are late in keeping tryst," said the Sheriff.

"'Twill not deny," answered Altoncroft, leaving his saddle and making a humble obeisance. "But, sooth to tell, my knaves broached a cask of double ale yesternight, and were loth to leave the dregs this morning. I crave your pardon, my lord Sheriff, and kiss your hand. And to the matter before us—I bring witnesses who, I think, will clearly establish my rights. I desire to have a free and fair decision, and will submit to it when it is pronounced; but I say frankly that if injustice be done me—"

"There shall be no injustice done either party," responded the Sheriff. "Proceed we to business: and I trust that no broil will break the amity of our meeting, but that all will respect this emblem of peace," pointing to the spear and glove, which his page held aloft. "Time wears on, and we shall proceed. Sergeants, proclaim and fence our court of arbitration."

One of the sergeants blew his horn thrice, and then made the proclamation, and "fenced the court" (as the phrase was) against all disturbance, which was denounced under high pains and penalties. The contending parties, mostly dismounted, were arranged on either side of the Arbiter, who elected to hear Altoncroft's evidence first. Altoncroft, like his opponent, had no documents of any kind to produce—his charters and sasines having long become non-existent, so that his case depended entirely upon what lawyers call parole proof. The monk, now on foot, and holding open his book, which was an old manuscript copy of the Gospels and richly illuminated, advanced to discharge the duty of administering the usual oath to the witnesses. This he did with all solemnity. Each man, when called in rotation, swore, with his right hand laid upon the sacred volume, and afterwards partook of a morsel of bread, and pronounced the imprecation that if he told an untruth the morsel might become mortal poison—a form probably borrowed from the Hebrew judicial procedure with the "water of jealousy."

The bulk of Altoncroft's proof, as expiscated chiefly by questions from the Sheriff, amounted somewhat to this—that the Laird's predecessors seemed to have always regarded the disputed ground, embracing a wide portion of the moorland on one side of the Deadman's Holm, as their own property, the burn being, to a considerable extent, the line of march. There were flaws in the witness-bearing, and much of it did not hang well together, as being inconclusive and sometimes contradictory hearsay. But Ballinshaw appeared to consider the proof as possessing a good deal of weight. When it came to his turn to adduce his witnesses, he whispered to Johnston, who was to be the first sworn—"Now comes the pinch, Edie; and for Gudesake dinna fail me! Thae Altoncroft rogues ha'e said ower muckle, and we maun damnify them, else we're lost. Dinna you mind the bit aith; it's just mere wind out o' your mouth. Ne'er scruple, lad, in your master's service. A fu' purse aye heals a troubled conscience. Stand up stoutly for my richt, and ding them a' doon. The lave o' our men will follow you like a wheen sheep louping a dyke."

"I daurna do mair than I ha'e promised, Laird, though it were for my ain faither," responded Edie, shaking his head. "But trust me, what I promised, and what I'll swear in the face o' the sun, will bear you out. Tak' nae fear."

The Sergeant's horn sounding again, Edie, assuming the firmest demeanour he could, laid down his spear, and presented himself for examination. He took the oath and the ordeal with becoming gravity, and then proceeded to depone how it consisted with his belief that the ground in question belonged to Ballinshaw. Edie swore that he had frequently heard his father, grandfather, and other discreet men, who knew the locality, say so: that this was the common understanding of the country: that he himself had often seen Ballinshaw hunt over the said portion of moorland. "And to make siccar," added he, "if your lordship will please to walk ower the ground alang wi' me, I will point out the true marches as they were aye considered."

This was the most matter-of-fact proposal which had been as yet offered, and it was readily accepted. Edie took his way, accompanied by nearly the whole of the assemblage. He made a wide circuit, inclining sometimes to the right and sometimes to the left. "The auld march rins this way, according to what I've heard, and according to what I ken," he repeatedly deponed. "I'm walking here on the land o' Ballinshaw. I swear, on soul and conscience, that the yird aneath my feet is Ballinshaw's sure and certain."

In this way he traversed a large space of the moorland, greatly to the satisfaction of his master, whose cunning eyes sparkled with joy. But the fiery Laird of Altoncroft, unable to control his chagrin longer, suddenly confronted the witness and bade him halt. The undaunted Johnston obeyed, folding his arms, and giving his interrupter a sarcastic scowl.

"Do you, sirrah, dare to swear that what you are pointing out are the true boundaries of my lands?" demanded Altoncroft.

"What cause is there to doubt his word?" cried Ballinshaw, pressing to the support of his hopeful witness. "Let the worthy Shirra judge."

"I tell you, Altoncroft," said the witness, drawing himself up to his full height; "I tell you, as I ha'e sworn, that all alang the yird o' Ballinshaw's land has been aneath my feet. Will that content you?"

"Mis-sworn villain!" ejaculated Altoncroft, furiously.

"I'm nae mis-sworn villain," retorted Johnston: "and were you and me here alane, wi' only the broom-bushes around us, I wad gar you eat back your foul words. I ha'e seen your back before this day, and I may see it again."

Altoncroft, stung by the retort, thrust his spear at the speaker's body, piercing the iron-plated jack. Johnston uttered a yell of mingled rage and pain, and staggering back under the shock, vainly attempted to unsheath his sword, and then dropped to the ground at full length. An applauding cheer from one party of the spectators, and a vengeful cry from another, boded a general conflict. Swords were drawn, and spears lowered, and warlike slogans arose amidst the tumult. Altoncroft, having withdrawn his lance, would have repeated his thrust, had not Ruthven Somervil, on the impulse of the moment, started forward, and baring his blade, strode across the prostrate man to save him from further assault. A dozen spears were levelled at the youth's breast, and as many advanced to protect him. The Sheriff spurred his horse into the press, and commanded all to keep the peace. His command had the effect of enforcing a pause.Chapter VII.

Aft trifles big mishanters bring,
Frae whilk a hunder mair may spring;
An' some, wha thrawart tempers ha'e,
Aft stand unkent in their ain way;

But aye, to guard against a coup,
Fowk should look weel afore they loup.

—Richard Gall—"The Tint Quey."

The fish shall never swim the flood,
Nor corn grow through the clay,
If the fiercest fire that ever was kindled
Twine me and Rothiemay.

—Ballad—"The Burning of Frendraught."

THE timely interposition of the Sheriff prevented the commission of more violence. "Back! Altoncroft!" cried he, whilst his men surrounded the fallen trooper, whom Ballinshaw, with trembling arms, was endeavouring to raise. "Draw off your followers, Altoncroft," continued Sir Robert. "You have broken Border faith, and insulted the representative of the law and the King."

Altoncroft, sullenly sheathing his dagger, answered with a growl—"The audacious falsehoods of this varlet would have moved patient Job; and I am not to be blamed."

"I swore no falsehoods, but gave leal and soothfast witnessing," retorted Johnston, who was now resting on his left elbow; "and this I'll also swear, that next time we meet in a fair field we shall not part thus," shaking his gauntleted right hand at his enemy.

"Come awa' oot o' this sturyfyke, master," whispered the gaberlunzie to Ruthven. "You stand in deadly peril; for Royston Scott is nae craw to shoot at. Come awa'."

He succeeded in drawing Ruthven out of the tumult. Altoncroft obeyed the Sheriff by leading his men back some space, and so allowed his victim's comrades to gather around him and do what they could to staunch his wound. Under the impression that the gentle Johnston was dying, the attendant priest pressed through the confusion, knelt on the grass at his side, and holding up a crucifix, prepared to shrive him; but Edie scouted the notion that his end was near.

"Dinna fear for me, holy father," he said, smiling grimly. "As broken a ship has come to land; and Death and me winna shake hands at this time o' day. And never think that I have perjured mysel'; for the sin o' perjury is not on my conscience. The ground is not Ballinshaw's, you say? I never made faith that it is. Bethink ye, holy father, o' my words. I swore that I stood on my master's ground; and so I did. Pull aff my boots, and you will find, in the soles o' them, an inch or twa o' earth from the yard o' Ballinshaw tower. *That* saves my conscience, and makes the matter but a jest: so if I am to die, I winna die with a falsehood in my mouth." He finished with a hollow laugh at the deception which he had practised.

At this juncture a horseman, with the royal cognizance, the rampant red lion, emblazoned on his breast, galloped up the side of the stream, and made directly towards the Sheriff, to whom he delivered a sealed packet. The knight cut asunder the silken strings that bound it, broke the seal, and opening the packet, eagerly scanned the paper which it contained. His cheek reddened, his eyes sparkled, and he bit his nether lip, then deliberately re-folding the document, which seemed to have given him both surprise and mortification, he handed a few coins to the messenger, who, after making dutiful acknowledgment, turned his horse, and rode off as rapidly as he had come.

"A strange revolution of Fortune's wheel," whispered the Sheriff to his chief attendant. "The King's Grace has appointed George Hepburn, the kinsman of Altoncroft, Sheriff in my room, and commends me to resign my office into his hands without delay, for which purpose he is to be at Jedburgh to-morrow at noon. This is the work of my unfriends at our fickle Sovereign's court. Altoncroft cannot yet know of the change, else he would spurn my authority and provoke strife: therefore, I must dismiss him at once. I should have arrested him when he stabbed the witness; but I feared that such action would only embroil the business still further; and I am now glad it was not done."

The Sheriff went over to Royston Scott, and said that after what had happened on the field, the arbitration proceedings behoved to be adjourned to some future day, and also enjoined him to retire, and to keep the peace. Altoncroft obeyed, and departed with his followers.

"There's the main danger blawn ower," said the gaberlunzie, viewing with much satisfaction the rude Laird's retreat. "We winna toom a tankard wi' the gentle Johnston the nicht; and wha kens whether he'll see the morn? We'll tak' the road, wi' your leave, master, as lang as the play is fair."

What road?—whither were they going? Ruthven indicated his intended destination, but did not desire to return to Greenholm, where he had changed his dress; and he added that he wished his route to be taken, so far as practicable, by paths not commonly frequented, to avoid any other mischance. The gaberlunzie was ready to accompany him by any route.

They left the Deadman's Holm without attracting much notice, and were speedily in the midst of solitudes. As the day wore to its close, they made a halt on the edge of a wood, and what Harthill's wallet yet contained, in the shape of viands, formed a substantial repast. This done, the journey was resumed while the sun was setting.

How red he glares amongst those deepening clouds,
Like the blood he predicts.

Soon, through the fading lustre above Sol's ocean-bed, Hesperus, the lover's star, sparkled brightly. Our wayfarer's path now led near a sluggish stream which skirted a hilly chain, and beyond the heights lay a village, where, as Harthill said, they might find lodgement for the night; but it had this disadvantage, that it was part of the barony pertaining to Altoncroft's kinsman, the newly-made Sheriff, and, therefore, Ruthven thought that their more prudent course would be to seek a less questionable place of rest. But, in short, to tell the truth, he was secretly desirous of parting, as soon as might be, with Willie, and of pursuing his course alone to Berwick, where he might obtain shipping for France—a country which afforded opportunities, to friendless and adventurous young Scots like himself of carving out their fortunes with their swords.

The twilight darkened, and the path grew wilder. Occasionally the harsh screams of birds of prey smote on the ear, and seemed to chill the gaberlunzie's blood.

"I dinna like the cries o' thae birds ava—they aye bode ill," he said. "Nae doubt they think to pyke our banes belyve. Shue! shue! ye evil emissaries! Our Lady help us! was yon a groan? Heard you naething, master?"

"It sounded like the fall of a fragment of rock from yonder cliff," answered Ruthven, with indifference.

Harthill shook his head, as if dubious of the explanation. His mind engrained with superstitious frailty, he began to hear uncanny sounds all around him. Every sough of the wind among the brackens was a dread presage. Hurrying his steps, he frequently left Ruthven in the rear; and to every half-jocular remonstrance of the youth, whose strength of limb was fast failing, Willie had but one apology:—

"It's a bogley part this after dark. I've heard as mony stories aboot ugsome sichts seen here as there's teeth in my head. I wadna put ower a nicht here, no for the crown o' Scotland. Haste you, master, haste you! It's for your ain gude."

Without doubt he meant well. But Ruthven flagged more and more, and, after climbing a grassy eminence, which was surmounted by the ruins of a place of strength, he protested that, happen what might, he would go no farther.

"You're in jest, master?" cried Harthill, scratching the side of his head in sheer vexation.

"We can rest here till daylight," replied Ruthven. "The place is lone, and therefore safe."

"Safe?" echoed Willie, with somewhat of asperity. "If we be sae daft as to rest here, we may ne'er see daylicht. Be advised, master, be advised."

Ruthven, however, was not to be advised. He advanced towards the ruin. The gaberlunzie followed with laggard pace, and shrank back when an owl started out, and, hooting dolefully, flew over their heads.

"There's a warning!" ejaculated Willie. "The place is fu' o' uncanny things. Come back, for ony sake."

But Ruthven still advanced. The ruin, in its palmy days, had consisted of a massive square tower of two storeys above the ground floor, with battlemented roof, and surrounded by an outer wall, which was now broken down to heaps of rubbish, overgrown with coarse vegetation. The roof had fallen in, and so had both floors, leaving only a shell of crumbling, grim walls: the courtyard was miry: and the arched portal preserved no vestige of the iron-bound door which had once barred passage. As Ruthven was about to pass inward, he was stayed for a moment by the almost hysterical entreaties of his companion, who now assumed a tone of wailing.

"I shall lodge here till morning," answered the youth determinedly. "If anything earthly molests me, I carry a stout heart and a trusty blade; and unearthly things I fear not."

The gaberlunzie held up his hands in deprecation of such a foolhardy resolve; but at length he said—"Aweel, master, a wilfu' man maun ha'e his ain way, and I maun leave you for the nicht. May a' haly saints watch ower you! I'll gang-on to the neist bigging, and in the morning I'll come back; but I fear the morning winna find you a living wicht."

"Never fear; but do as you say," responded Ruthven. "Take this small guerdon"—bestowing some money. "You'll find me in the morning hale and sound. Good-night, and good luck."

The gaberlunzie was loth to part; but his superstitious nature prevailed, and he took leave, reiterating his promise to return in the morning.

Ruthven entered the ruined pile. The interior was heaped with fallen stones and debris. Casting his eye upward, as from the bottom of a deep well, he saw the dim welkin overhead, which was becoming sprinkled with golden cressets.

Star after star, from some unseen abyss,
Came through the sky, like thoughts into the mind,
We know not whence.

Some square apertures in the walls, which once were windows, were partly choked with grass: a narrow stone stair had given access to the first storey, but only a few of the lower steps remained intact: the air felt damp and chill, and the pervading silence was like that of a sepulchre. Ruthven weariedly sat down on a hillock of ruin close to the portal, and bending his face upon his hands, fell into a reverie, which eventually lapsed into troubled slumber.

When he awoke from a confused dream, trembling with cold, all was dark around him. He arose and went out into the courtyard to look at the sky. It was cloudless, and bright with the celestial host; and a gusty breeze blew from the west. As he turned in that direction, he perceived, upon the verge of the horizon, a glimmering light, which rose and fell alternately, but in short space grew into a broad and steady glare. Was "yon red glare the western star?" or was it "the beacon-blaze of war?" Whatever it was, it speedily became an intense mass of flame, shedding a lurid gleam on earth and heaven.

As Ruthven watched the mysterious fire, the clatter of horses approaching from the west struck his ear. He receded into the portal, and drew his sword. In a few moments several horsemen, riding in disorder, broke dimly on his view as they ascended the height. Up they came: they urged their panting steeds over the rubbish of the wall, and drew rein in the courtyard. They were five in number, all wearing warlike harness, and seemed to have fled from an unsuccessful fight. Four dismounted, but the remaining one kept his saddle, and gazed back to the distant blaze, which was now sinking.

"Woe worth this nicht, that has seen mair ruin wrought than can be repaired in a lang life time!" ejaculated this rider, wringing his hands. "That cruel spoiler! that bluid-thirsty riever! Curses on him that wad fire an auld man's house aboon his head!"

Ruthven recognised the voice as that of Lauder of Ballinshaw.

"A stranger here! a lurking enemy!" exclaimed one of the party, spying Ruthven in the doorway; but instantly Ruthven called out that he was no enemy but a friend to Ballinshaw.

"By St. Bryde! this is the brave lad that defended our Edie when he fell!" cried the man, "Of a surety he is a friend."

Ruthven, assured of safety, stepped out of the portal, and sheathing his brand, hastened to the old Laird's side, inquiring what had befallen; but the question had to be thrice repeated ere Lauder seemed to hear and comprehend it, and then he started, and peering down into Ruthven's face, exclaimed—"Wha is this?"

"The stranger who defended our Edie," said the retainer who had previously spoken.

"Indeed!" said Ballinshaw, in a vague way, and again directing his eye towards the fading fire. "See yonder what's befaun. Bluidshed and murder! Ruth and ruin! A' is lost—the airn kist fu' o' merks in the secret closet ahint the spence—the candlesticks and the plate that my great-grandsire brought frae the Low Countries—a' plundered—a' gane. But how cam' you here, lad?"

"Night overtook me on my way, and I sought shelter here, where scant shelter there is," replied Ruthven.

"We seek refuge, too," said the retainer; "but if Altoncroft be in pursuit o' us—"

"Altoncroft!" cried Ruthven. "Is he the ravager?"

"Ay," returned the man. "His hatred has burnt up Ballinshaw. When we reached hame yesterday, word was heard that our fickle King had appointed Altoncroft's kinsman Sheriff, in room o' the just Sir Robert Home; and we heard the news like our death-knell. Dreading the warst, as weel we micht, we prepared the auld house for defence—armed every man and callant—and keepit strict watch. Afore midnicht, Altoncroft cam' wi' a' his power. There was a fierce and deadly struggle; but he brak' in wi' his ruthless band, and we were driven out, and the place was fired. The flames lichted our way as we fled."

"Did Edie Johnston perish in the struggle?" asked Ruthven.

"Not that I can tell," said the retainer. "When the enemy brak' in, we lowered Edie into the subterranean passage that leads frae the ha' to the middle o' the garden; but if the villains discovered his hiding place, they would gi'e him but short shrift."

NOTE.—A parallel to the catastrophe of the arbitration is recorded in Sir John Sinclair's "*Statistical Account of Scotland*" (Vol. V., 153), as having occurred in the parish of Menmuir, in the county of Forfar:—

"Two lairds quarrelled about their marches, and witnesses were brought to swear to the old boundaries. One of these chieftains, provoked to hear his opponent's servant declare, on oath, that he then stood on his master's ground, pulled a pistol from his belt, and shot him dead on the spot. It was found that to save his conscience he had earth in his shoes brought from his laird's lands."

"A' my strength is blasted like a flower o' the field, and a' my gear gane like snaw aff a dyke," moaned Ballinshaw, again wringing his hands. "But the enemy may be hard ahint us, and we maun on and awa'—on and awa'."

"Our horses are blawn, and we maun gi'e them some minutes' rest," said the retainer, languidly laying himself on a heap of rubbish.

Scarcely had they thought of rest when the clatter of hoofs sounded in the glen below. Ballinshaw started in affright, and the next moment had fallen from his steed, a victim of apoplexy.

"'Tis Royston Scott!" exclaimed one of his retainers. "We are but dead men!"

The pursuers, headed by Altoncroft, rapidly began to ascend the hill. Leading his followers, Scott encouraged them in their work with promise of reward. Ruthven Somervil watched their movements, and, lifting a large stone, cast it down upon Altoncroft with so sure an aim that it struck horse and man to the earth. For the moment there was panic among Scott's supporters, but an instant later, having left their leader to recover as best he might, they made for the crest of the hill, all eyes ablaze with vengeance against the youth who had thrown their master.

Ruthven wisely decided on flight. Entering the ruined fort, he dragged himself up on the broad sill of one of the windows, and leapt upon the soft, boggy ground beneath, seized one of the horses, and galloped away. Shouts and cries were behind him; he pricked his horse with his dagger for want of spurs, and dashed among the mountains, never drawing rein until he considered himself safe from the reach of the anger of the house of Altoncroft.

CHAPTER VIII.

"The star of the unconquered will,
He rises in my breast,
Serene and resolute and still,
And calm and self-possessed."

LITTLE did Ruthven Somervil reck that Edie Johnston, whom he had so valiantly defended, was the man who had slipped him through the portal of Hawksglen on that long-past night. Had a suspicion, even hinting at that, dawned upon him, he would have instantly sought out Edie and tried to learn from him something of his descent. With Johnston and kindred spirits he was destined to have much in common, but the question of his parentage was never mentioned in their hearing.

Ruthven found refuge at Hunterspath, a notorious Border-raiders' stronghold. The tidings he brought of the outrage on Ballinshaw, and his modest recital of the part he himself had played in recent events, won the sympathy and admiration of the mosstroopers, and he soon proved his daring before their own eyes. None was more fearless than Ruthven, no sword on all the Borders was sharper than his, and when, at the end of two years, the Chief of Hunterspath went down to his robber grave as the result of a treacherous thrust from a foeman's spear, Ruthven Somervil was hailed as his successor. To him was assigned the Captaincy by common consent, and never a man went back on his choice.

The daring life of a mosstrooper did not ill agree with Ruthven's valiant spirit. He was never more in his element than when leading his men across the English Border on some mission of pillage, and never prouder than when he withdrew into the stronghold of Hunterspath to share his spoils with his companions.

But sometimes, when alone, a kindly thought of Eleanor Elliot brought a mist to his eyes as he considered how ill-suited a Border-raider was to be a mate of such a gentle lady. From the topmost turret of his own keep he would gaze in the direction of Hawksglen, and try to discern the towers of the ancient castle where his childhood and youth had been passed.

"Some day, some day," he would sigh, "God grant that I may clasp my fair angel to my breast."

Since the morning when he had said good-bye to Sir James and Lady Elliot, more than three years ago, no word had ever passed between him and Eleanor. But something told him that the fair daughter of Hawksglen, who had looked into his eyes with the eyes of affection, was true to his undeclared love, and would yet welcome him to her arms. Had he known that Lady Elliot was assiduously endeavouring to arrange a marriage between Eleanor and Sir Anthony Maxwell of Rutherwell, it would have filled him with alarm, but even knowledge of that kind would not have shaken his faith in the companion of his early years. One summer evening, when he was more than usually moody, the long-desired opportunity of seeing Hawksglen came in his way. Edie Johnston burst in upon the mosstroopers.

"The English loons are owre again!" he exclaimed. "Sir Dacre de Ermstein and twa hunder o' his men are spreading disaster on every hand. I hear that Elliot's place is the next mark for them."

"Elliot? Hawksglen?" queried Ruthven, as he sprang to his feet.

"Ay, the very same," replied Edie.

"Then to-night we must strike a blow for the honour of Scotland. The quarrel of Elliot shall be our quarrel, and God help the English loon that fa's in our way."

A few minutes later, at the head of his followers, Ruthven Somervil was advancing rapidly towards Hawksglen. Already news of the attack from the English enemy had spread in the district, and barons and their retainers, from different quarters, had assembled to help Elliot, and resist their common foe. When Ruthven and his men appeared upon the scene the conflict was at its height. Sir Anthony Maxwell, cheered by the thought that Eleanor's hand might be the reward of his valour, fought nobly for the house of Elliot. But it was evident that Sir Dacre de Ermstein was to be victor. Once or twice the defenders had been forced back, and the spirits of the garrison began to droop. Then came the turn in fortune's wheel. The reivers burst through the lines, and changed the fate of Hawksglen.

Another half-hour and the defeat of the English was complete. Horse and foot broke away from the fatal conflict, and fled for refuge in every direction. A murmur of rage broke from the lips of Ermstein, and he turned to one of his followers.

"This robber chief—his name?" he demanded.

"Ruthven Somervil. He keeps the Tower of Hunterspath with a powerful and desperate band."

"Ruthven Somervil," said the knight slowly; "he shall be remembered. Chance may yet throw vengeance into my power. But Elliot may thank his robber allies, for, had not they come to his aid, the flag of Dacre de Ermstein would now have been floating triumphantly over the towers of Hawksglen."

Giving vent to his anger in these and similar words, the English knight withdrew his forces, and retired in the direction of the Border. The raiders of Hunterspath, greedy of booty, did not hesitate to despoil the English dead, and went about their business, while the servants of Hawksglen succoured those who had been wounded in defence of their house.

Sir James Elliot invited Maxwell, and others who had come to his relief, to partake of his hospitality, and Lady Elliot was most assiduous in her attentions to the guests.

"The chief of Hunterspath," she said to her husband, as she noticed that Ruthven was not in the banqueting hall.

"Ay; I had almost forgotten," returned Sir James, as he went in search of the mosstrooper.

A moment later he held his breath in wonder: Eleanor and Ruthven were in conversation in the courtyard. The mosstrooper's visor was still down, as it had been during the fight. Sir James approached.

"You will drink to the defeat of our foes?" he said.

"Nay, Sir James," and the voice sounded strangely familiar in his ear. "With Sir Dacre de Ermstein vowing vengeance against me I have other things to think of. But judge me not a churl," he went on, as he took Eleanor's hand; "one touch from your daughter's fingers, and one glance from her flashing eye, are reward enough for the Captain of Hunterspath."

CHAPTER IX.

Wha's friends, wha's faes, in this cauld warld,
Is e'en richt ill to learn;
But an evil e'e hath looked on thee,
My bonnie, bonnie bairn.

A. M'Laggan.

WHEN Ruthven mounted his steed, and passed the gate of Hawksglen, he found that all his followers, with the exception of Edie Johnston, had retired. Laden with booty, they had made tracks for Hunterspath, well knowing that their Captain was able to defend himself from the attack of any English straggler.

"It's a bonnie sicht," said Edie, as he indicated the English dead, "them a' lying heids and thraws. An' it was a bonnier sicht to see the lads gae aff wi' the plunder."

But Ruthven was in no mood for conversation. He had learned from Eleanor that Lady Elliot was desirous of marrying her to Sir Anthony Maxwell, and he well knew that Maxwell's valour that day must have greatly advanced him in the eyes of Hawksglen. Deep in thought—almost unconscious of the presence of Edie—he rode on, while the shades of night descended upon them.

By and by the friendly light of a wayside tavern burst upon their view, and roused Ruthven from his stupor. Edie watched the Captain's eyes light upon the inn.

"It's dry wark ridin' in silence," he ventured to remark.

"Ay, Edie, ay, but I had thoughts that kept me frae thirst."

"Ye've been unco quiet sin' ye left Hawksglen. What ails ye, gin I may mak' bold to speir?"

They had alighted from their steeds. Ruthven put his hand on Edie's shoulder.

"Twa men and a'e woman," he said, in a low tone.

"The auld complaint," answered Edie; "put yer sword in him. Wha is he?"

"Sir Anthony Maxwell."

"Him that ettles to mairry Elliot's dochter?"

"Ay, the same. And, Edie, I love the lass. I lived—it's a secret, and I give it to you alone—for twenty years at Hawksglen, and I loved Eleanor from childhood."

"Ay, twenty 'ear," repeated Edie, "you're the lad—"

"That was left one night with nothing but this," and he touched a little golden reliquary that hung round his neck, "to tell who I was."

Edie looked keenly at his Captain. Would he tell him there and then that he was the man who had passed him through the portal of Hawksglen, and tell him whence was his origin? Would he?—

Before he had time to do aught, his arms were pinioned behind his back, and three stout Englishmen had thrown themselves suddenly on Ruthven.

The assault was so unexpected and sudden that neither the Captain of Hunterspath nor Edie could offer the least resistance. Amid the jeers of their captors they were mounted on their horses. Sir Dacre de Ermstein rode up to Ruthven and whispered in his ear:

"The robber of Hunterspath shall not always prevail against the house of Ermstein."

By an ill-turn of Fortunes wheel the man who had beaten off the English foe from Hawksglen was now in the hands of that same foe—the victor led off in bonds by the vanquished!

A long night ride saw the forces of Sir Dacre de Ermstein across the Border, and on the afternoon of the following day the towers of Warkcliff Castle rose before Sir Dacre and his followers.

The Lady of Warkcliff, the childless wife of Sir Dacre de Ermstein, was sitting at her chamber window, vacantly watching the conflict that raged in the bosom of the sweet valley, between the heavy morning mists and the sun and wind. Lady de Ermstein had come of a noble English line: in her youth she had been peerless for her charms, but middle-age had reft all those youthful charms away; still, she was a stately dame, and still possessed those graces of manner which had so much enhanced her youthful beauty. But she was childless. This was the secret sorrow that preyed everlastingly upon her soul. Her husband was the last of his ancient line. With him would perish the noble house of De Ermstein, and the lordly domains of Warkcliff would pass away to the stranger.

Watching the battle in the valley between the mists and the sun and wind, she thought of that great cloud which had heavily enveloped her heart and hopes so long, which no sun, no breath of promise, would ever dissipate. Her husband burst into the chamber. His countenance was flushed, and his eye kindling, and his look elated. The lady had heard the tumult in the castle, but it only cost her a passing thought.

"Such tidings as I have to tell, Alice!" he exclaimed, grasping her by both hands. "Such tidings as make my heart leap!"

"They are not of sorrow, then!" said the lady, with a wan smile.

"No! why of sorrow? I have won a proud triumph, Alice. Mountjoy, whom I despatched to watch the Scots at their Weaponschaw, or military muster of the shire, has captured the villain Somervil, the robber who keeps a tower on the Cheviot hills, who infests the whole English marches, Mountjoy has made *him* a prisoner."

"And brought him to the castle?"

"Yes; and the mosstrooper now lies in the Donjon with iron on wrist and ankle."

"He has troubled the Border long," said the lady thoughtfully. "But you do not resolve to have his life?" she added, looking full in her husband's face.

"I have determined that he shall suffer the penalty due to his crimes," cried Sir Dacre; "and that within three days. Has he not been my relentless foe, the relentless spoliator of my lands? I never can forget that, through him, I suffered that disgraceful repulse before the tower of Hawksglen, which, but for his interposition, would have yielded to the assaults of my gallant soldiers. No, no, Alice, speak not a word for him; I will hear no petition from human lips that his life should be spared. Since the day at Hawksglen how often have my vassals been plundered and slain by the mosstroopers of Hunterspath? I will not listen to appeals for mercy to this noted outlaw—this villain whose pride and boast it is to plunder the domains of Warkcliff, and mortify their lord."

"But, husband," entreated the gentle-hearted lady, "resolve upon nothing until your passion has cooled down. Your spirits are flushed at this moment. There is no knightly virtue so brilliant as that of compassion for the vanquished foe."

"But what a foe this is, Alice," said the knight, "a mosstrooper—an outlawed and broken man—a miscreant who lives upon spoliation and rapine. *He* can claim no compassion."

"Still, to put him to death, miscreant as he is, may bring the vengeance of his confederates on the Scottish side upon you, husband.

Consider this: his death may add another to the many grounds of feud and fray which the turbulent Scottish chiefs have against you. And we have suffered much from the hatred of the Border Scots."

"It does not move my compassion for this ruffian," returned the knight, with a dark gloom on his brow, "thus to rake up the memories of our past wrongs and sorrows. Can I forget that, through the fell hatred of some caitiff-Scot, we are this day childless and heirless?"

"Childless, indeed!" sighed the lady, as, with a burst of grief, she sank on her husband's shoulder and wept aloud.

Sir Dacre was equally affected, but he forbore all signs of woe. He essayed to soothe his weeping wife, and laid her gently into a chair.

"Ay," said the knight, as he moodily perambulated the room, "Scottish hatred has struck at the root of our house, and will behold its extinction in a few short years. The house of De Ermstein traces its long descent from the chivalrous Norman who followed the Conqueror, and shared in the perils and glories of the field of Hastings. And shall this long line terminate with *me*? Alas! my name shall be erased for ever from the princely roll of English nobles."

"O, that child—that lost, lost child!" sobbed the weeping lady. "Twenty years have deepened the sad wound of my soul!"

"Childless, heirless," resumed Sir Dacre. "And this old house to close with me? One of my ancestors received the praise of King Edward on the field of Falkirk, where the Scottish rebels were scattered; another did his devoir gallantly under bold King Hall at Agincourt; and a third stabbed down the hump-backed Richard on Bosworth. We have all our ancient baronial honours about us. But oblivion is destined to swallow up all!"

"Let this outlaw live," cried the lady, starting from the chair, and clasping her husband's hands. "Shed no blood that may cry from the ground against us. Vengeance is the prerogative of Heaven alone. We who are in the midst of sorrow, who have no prospects but dark ones, we should excel in deeds of mercy. Let him live, keep him captive all his days, but shed no blood. I implore his life, husband; I implore it from the bottom of my heart."

The knight beheld her with amazement.

"Alice," he said calmly, "your feelings overpower you. This outlaw *must* suffer. I am here in the stead of the minister of Justice, who shall perform my duty."

CHAPTER X.

But young Beichan was a Christian born,
    And still a Christian was he,
Which made them put him in prison strang,
    And cauld and hunger sair to dree,
And fed on nocht but bread and water,
    Until the day that he mot dee.

—Lord Beichan.

ON being taken from the courtyard, Ruthven Somervil was, without delay, committed to close ward in the Donjon-keep. The armourer of the castle brought a pair of heavy chains, which he rivetted upon the prisoner's wrists and ankles, and secured the ends to a ring in the wall. The prison cell was low, small, and dark; two narrow loop-holes scarcely admitted the feeblest light. The captive heard, with a shudder, the bolts and bars drawn upon the door, and hammers driving them securely into their staples, and chains fastened across the door as an additional security.

Oppressed with the weight of his fetters, and more so by the insupportable weight of his disaster and despair, the outlaw sank down upon the floor of the cell, and lay for a long period silent and inert in body and soul. Consciousness scarce seemed within him. To look upon his motionless figure one would have thought him dead.

Almost involuntarily he raised his hand to his breast and felt, with a thrill of joy and sadness, the little reliquary found on his neck when left at the gate of Hawksglen, which still hung at his heart. For many years Elliot kept this mysterious trinket carefully locked up in his cabinet, and had refused to part with it even upon the urgent solicitations of Ruthven previous to his quitting the castle. But, after he joined the band of Hunterspath, Lady Eleanor contrived to gain possession of the trinket, unknown to her father, and, at an interview which she granted to her outlaw lover on the banks of the lake, she delivered it into his hands. Around his neck he had worn it ever since, and he was resolved to go to the grave with it. He now drew forth the little trinket, and, surveying it for a moment in the dim light, pressed it to his lips, for the sweet memory of her from whose hands he had received it as a love-gift. How his soul, as it roamed through the memories of the past, dwelt upon that meeting near the lake, as a weary traveller of the desert lingers long on the bosom of the green, shady oasis, with its glancing springs and flowing waters.

And this was an oasis in his life; before, behind, around it was all the desert in its barrenness. His soul recalled that autumn eve, with all its beauty and sweetness. Yonder shone the lake in the fading glories of the western sky. Eleanor was standing beneath the whispering shade of hazel, and he stood by her side, gazing on the fair young face that drooped with emotion; the mantling blush on the smooth cheek, the drooping of the eyelids, the bosom that heaved with sad and joyful thoughts, the lovely being whose heart was his, whose hand was pledged to him.

The captivity, the prison, the chains, the prospect of death, all were forgotten in the vision which the golden reliquary called magically into being.

But the "visioned scene" fled, like a delusive mirage, and, as it dissipated, it left the dungeon and the chains revealed and felt. The captive had left the oasis for ever, and was now in the midst of the waste, howling desert, horrors behind, and before, and around! Pent up within the four grim walls, only to be led forth to hear his doom, and thence to the place of death—a chained and powerless victim, prostrate beneath the uplifted, menacing hand of Destiny. Plunged in deepest despair, not a ray of hope could penetrate such a dungeon or such a despairing heart. The last sands of a troubled life were running out fast. And this was to be the end of him who was nursed in the lap of luxury, on whose career the crimes of others had cast a baleful influence. This the end of him who had gained fair Eleanor's heart. Alas for Eleanor!

The mental stupor returned, he lay sluggish on the ground; the little golden reliquary had lost its magic power. Like him who languished in the vaults of Chillon, he could have said—

"I had not strength to stir or strive,
But felt that I was still alive."

And there was freedom on the green heights of Cheviot, on the wide Border which he rode so long, in the halls of Hunterspath, where he had defied all power and every enemy. But he was a captive, chained to the wall like a dog. The time wore by unheeded; a ray of sunlight trembled into the cell, and vanished, and the wind began to blow—the wind that sounded high on Cheviot. The captive still sat grovelling on the ground.

He had a fancy that the door of the dungeon was hammered open, that a glare of torchlight illuminated the place, that voices arose, that forms passed before him.

"He is in despair," said one voice; and another answered: "He well may be so, for on the third morning he dies."

And then something like a laugh echoed through the cell.

"I will leave the food for him," said a voice again. "He will wake and be glad of it."

And the other voice said:

"Pity that so comely a youth should have followed the lawless career of a robber. In his King's service he might now have been a knight, and they say of him that he comes of noble blood."

"That is why our good lady pleads so strongly for his life."

"But she pleads in vain," said the other voice. "Sir Dacre's purpose is fixed. Noble or ignoble, this robber leader shall die; and the Border will be quiet after it. I will leave the bread and water."

And there was a drawing and hammering of bolts, and the clanking of chains, and then silence. And the captive awoke as from a dream, and saw the bread and water on the cold floor, near where he lay. The bitterness of his captivity was coming.

CHAPTER XI.

"When purposed vengeance I forego,
Term me a wretch, nor deem me foe;
And when an insult I forgive,
Then brand me as a slave, and live."

—*Rokeby.*

ON the following forenoon the captive outlaw was brought up from his cell to be confronted with De Ermstein, in the great hall of the castle. When the myrmidons intimated this to Somervil all his dejection and helplessness left him; he scorned that, in this his trying hour, an enemy should behold him cast down by misfortune, or in despair at the apprehension of a speedy death. Summoning all his daring courage, he became indifferent to whatever fate might await him; and he followed his keepers with a firm step and a flashing eye.

In an antique chair, set upon the *dais* or elevation at the upper end of the spacious hall, sat the stern knight of Warkcliff, attended by an imposing array of armed retainers. The deepest stillness prevailed when the prisoner appeared and was led up to the foot of the *dais*. Those who anticipated exultation at the sight of his misery were greatly deceived; they were startled on beholding his fearless mien and deportment. His face was calm but stern; and his eye met that of De Ermstein, but never quailed. He could not have displayed more bravery had he then stood upon the battlements of Hunterspath, with all his wild band around him. Not all the power of De Ermstein—not all the horrors of approaching death—could daunt him in a moment when faint-heartedness would have been deep disgrace.

"You have dragged me hither," began the outlaw, in a firm, measured tone, "to speak the doom which you are impatient to utter."

"You are here," answered Sir Dacre, standing up, "to receive that doom which your life of rapine makes justice. The sufferings of my vassals, whom you so frequently have despoiled, call for redress at my hands, and upon your head. I gratify no private malice, no private feud, in pronouncing judgment of death upon a villain who stands outlawed by both kingdoms. And the terror of such a judgment may have a salutary effect upon the many lawless ruffians who infest the marches, and, by their depredations, give constant causes for disturbing the peace of these kingdoms."

"By destroying my life," replied the outlaw—"a life placed at your mercy by an act of the foulest treachery—you shall gratify your own malice more than redress the sufferings of your dependants. To you, Sir Dacre, I have long been a personal and detested foe. The defeat at Hawksglen can never be obliterated from your memory; the disgraceful rout of the predatory forces, under your command, rankles yet in your breast, and has stained your escutcheon, which has been still more indelibly stained by the deed of treachery and ruffian guile which threw me into your power—"

He was here interrupted by the clamour of the attendants; the jailor even placed his hand upon his mouth to stop his speech; and some cried out to dash his brains against the wall for such insolence to such a knight. Sir Dacre himself was confounded by the audacity of the mosstrooper's speech; but his high pride conquered his indignant emotions, and, affecting to smile, he imposed silence upon his retainers, and forbade any one to interfere, either by word or deed, in what should follow.

"I thank you, Sir Dacre," cried the captive, "for silencing the empty clamour of your armed serfs. I have much to say, and I will not be overborne by insolent tumult. On you, Sir Dacre de Ermstein, I charge treachery and fraud unworthy of the last scion of the noble house of Warkcliff. I have defied you behind the battlements of Hawksglen, on the field of your defeat—defied you as a soldier and a freeman should—but never did I stoop to treachery and fraud to gain an advantage over my foe."

"How, churl! of what fraud speak you?" demanded Sir Dacre.

"The fraud which rivetted these chains on my limbs," answered Somervil, elevating his fettered hands. "It was fraud so dastardly and so base that it will ever cover you with shame, and expose you to the deep scorn of all whose hearts are warmed by feelings of honour."

"Thou art beyond the pale of honour as well as of law," retorted De Ermstein, with a blush on his hard face. "To what code of honour, observed by thyself, canst *thou* appeal? Wretch, this insolence, this show of frontless audacity, will avail thee nothing save to hasten thy doom. It is my sentence that upon the third morning hence thou shalt hang at the cross of Warkcliff!"

An approving hum and murmur broke from the attendant soldiery, and there came a momentary palor over the captive's face; but it was the result of a mere evanescent emotion, and soon passed away.

"Hear me, Sir Dacre," he exclaimed, with passionate ardour. "You have pronounced my doom, and that doom I am ready to meet. The prospect of the speedy approach of death has terrors in it for those only who have found life pleasant, and who bask under the smile of fortune, and stand high and fair in the world, who have kindred and loving friends, who have wealth and luxury to leave behind them. To such the fear of death is terrible. But I, who, from my ill-fated birth, have been the sport of destiny, I have nothing to fear from the repose of the grave; and there was mercy with Heaven even for the thief who hung quivering in his death-agony on the cross. But flatter not yourself, noble knight, that, by my murder, you shall relieve yourself of a stern and unbending foe. I never was your foe until patriotism called me to the field to oppose your inroad upon the Border. And my enmity to the enemy of my country shall live after me. My followers will deeply revenge my death. Hang me upon a gallows high as Haman's if you will; and each night your lady shall set her hood by the blaze of your burning villages. From one end of the wide domains of Warkcliff to the other shall ravage and destruction spread. And when, in the midst of ruth, and rapine, and bloodshed, you shall stand aghast, powerless against foes whose power you can neither break nor resist, you will then think on the evil day when Ruthven Somervil died!"

Lost in thought, De Ermstein waved his hand involuntarily; and the jailor, taking that to be a sign for the removal of the prisoner, hurried him away.

The attendants hovered about for some minutes, and then noiselessly left the hall, leaving their lord standing solitary on the *dais*.

A light footstep approached, and, looking up, Sir Dacre beheld his lady. She was in great agitation, and came up to his chair, and, taking him by the hand, said:

"Have you doomed the outlaw to death?"

"I have," answered Sir Dacre. "I could, in justice, pronounce no other doom."

"I beheld him through yonder window," she said, "and never did I behold a nobler-looking youth. With what grace and courage he confronted you; what emotion in his countenance; what defiance in his tone. Such a youth must not die so shameful a death. I thought, as I looked upon him, of our own boy."

"Peace, Alice; you kindle afresh the embers of pain," cried Sir Dacre. "Recall not the memory of that one dread sorrow which has for ever destroyed our happiness."

"Grant me this captive's life," she cried passionately.

"Do *you* plead for him?"

"I plead and pray that he may be spared to forsake his evil career, and seek his fortune in some honourable path. It is hard that so young and so noble a stranger should die, and by our hands. Give him life, husband, though you may not give him liberty. His life is the boon I crave. Deny me not."

"I would deny it, Alice, to the mother that bore him," said De Ermstein, with stern composure, "though she pled for him on her bended knees. I dare not suffer such a villain to live. Did I spare him, I might be accused of participation in his crimes. Plead for him no more; I am inexorable. I am steeled against pity."

CHAPTER XII.

"The last, the fatal hour is come
That bears my love from me;
I hear the death-note of the drum,
I mark the gallows tree.
The bell has toll'd; it shakes my heart;
The trumpet speaks thy name;
And must my Gilderoy depart
To bear a death of shame?"

—*Campbell.*

THE watery sun of the third morning slowly dispelled the mists that filled the vale of Warkcliff. Although the day was only yet in its infancy, one would have thought, from seeing the crowd, that all the denizens of the village and all the peasantry from the surrounding domains had gathered in the open market place. Great numbers of the rustics were armed; and parties of troopers, in De Ermstein's pay, pranced up and down, quelling disturbance, and maintaining order.

That concourse had assembled to behold the mosstrooper die. The busy hammer of the artisan was heard sounding on the gibbet, which was in course of erection in the centre of the market. It was finished after much labour, and the workmen sat down at the foot of it, and, throwing by their tools, partook heartily of bread and ale, which they shared with some few notorious topers of the village who gathered round them. Healths were drunk, and jests bandied about from mouth to mouth, as if at some merry festival; troops of urchins romped around the gibbet; mothers held up children in their arms to see it; and every window was open and filled with eager faces. The armed men began to gather in close ranks around the scene of death, and the crowd increased.

And now the bell in the old steeple began to toll, announcing the hour of death. The sound of trumpets from the castle denoted that the prisoner had been brought up from his cell. The gates were flung open, and the cavalcade of death issued forth. Every murmur of the crowd was hushed. Every eye was turned toward that grim procession. Amidst a strong force of horsemen and footmen, under the personal leadership of Sir Dacre, appeared the condemned outlaw. A cart, covered with black cloth, and drawn by a sorry nag, stood near the gate. The hangman sat at the head of it, in a grim dress, and having his face hidden by a black vizard. The captive ascended the cart with the assistance of a tall monk, who also followed him into it, and seemed preparing him for death.

Somervil's chains were away, but his hands were bound at his back by a thick cord. His head was bare, and his long tresses flowed on his shoulders, or blew in the gale. Not a shade of fear was perceptible upon his calm countenance; his step never faltered; not a tremor ran through a limb. He rose superior to his cruel doom. This fearful end to his career had lost its usual terrors, and nothing could shake his stoical courage and defiant haughtiness.

The bell still tolled! The sandglass of the outlaw's life was fast running out. If he had one painful emotion, it was when he thought of Eleanor and the hopes of his heart, which were now withered and destroyed. *She* would hear of his sad fate, and mourn long without consolation; but she would never behold his grave.

The bell tolled! And he who had striven for years to pierce the dark mystery of his lineage was to die, and the secret to be impenetrable. What frightful iniquity lay on the head of those who had reft him from his parents' arms, and brought him to a death like this. The hope of his whole life was to discover his parentage, and to assume his own just rank; but how had such a hope been crushed! And he would die, ignorant of the mother at whose breast he hung.

The bell tolled! And when he beheld the crowd, and the armed men, and the tall gibbet, and the open windows, fierce thoughts rushed like furies through his heart. His death-scene was to be a holiday spectacle; he was to be butchered, like the Gladiator of the Colosseum, to make a holiday. O, how he thought of some grim night, of rain and storm and darkness, when the wild bands of Cheviot would burst upon Warkcliff and make it blaze to heaven!

The bell tolled! The shade of Eleanor again! The memory of the gentle being who loved him! His thoughts could not forsake *her*! And how his death would break her heart!

On with the procession! On to the spot of death. Let the bell toll, and the trumpets blow, and the crowd shout. The prisoner was still undaunted. Not all the triumph and the malice of his foes could shake his stern composure.

He sat down in the cart beside the monk, who, with his missal open, was muttering in a low tone, indistinctly heard by the prisoner, but unheeded by him. The hangman sat watching them twain. But the monk was so tall, so darkly cowled, so gaunt, and so repulsive. What he read, or what he muttered, no one knew. He might have been muttering fiendish spells.

The horsemen in front cleared away the crowd before the slowly-rolling cart. The murmuring of the crowd broke out afresh, and men pressed and fought forward, and children were held high up to look at *him;* and women gazed keenly, and, turning to each other, said how handsome he was, and so noble was his look. A sound of pity here and there was drowned in the general noise; the guards called out for open room, and horses pranced and bore back the eager spectators. And swords and spears flashed, and feathers waved and danced, and the cart slowly rolled on, bearing its doomed burden.

It rolled on slowly, and then stopped beneath the gibbet. The place of death was reached. The rope hung dangling to and fro, and swaying in the wind. The hangman rose and put forth his hand to seize it, but the wind was so strong that he could not come near it for many minutes, and this little incident furnished food for jest and laughter. He at length caught it and made a noose.

The outlaw stood up lightly and looked around with an unmoved countenance. Some seemed to be of the belief that he meant to address the crowd; but it was not so. The bell ceased. Far down the valley the old battle still waged between the morning mist and the sun and wind, and the outlaw cast a long glance down the valley to descry the distant hills of Cheviot; but, until the sun and wind had vanquished their enemy, the blue hills of Cheviot could not be seen.

The hangman now approached the captive with the noosed rope in his hand. Somervil involuntarily shuddered at the approach of that dingy-looking, vizarded miscreant; but by that hideous miscreant's hands he must die.

CHAPTER XIII.

"I curse the hand that did the deed,
The heart that thocht the ill;
The feet that bore me wi' sic speed
The comely youth to kill."

—*Gil Morice.*

DIE!

Not while there was a hand to save! Not while there was keen steel unsheathing to break the captive's bonds! Not while there was a power to control evil destiny, and blast the malice of the remorseless De Ermstein. Die? The star of Ruthven Somervil was in the ascendant, swiftly culminating.

What sound was that which rose from the swaying concourse? What sight was that which startled the grim executioner? The blast of a horn, and the drawing of a dagger by the priest. Somervil was no less startled. The priest had thrown down his missal and drawn a dagger, and, with deadly spring, he struck the dagger through the executioner, who, with a piercing howl, fell heavily on his face in the cart. To recover his steel from the body of the howling hound, and to cut the outlaw's bonds asunder was, to the intrepid priest, but the work of an instant, and Somervil was free. Free, and thus environed by the armed bands of De Ermstein? Yes; for from every side dashed forward numbers of mounted rustics, well armed, who, trampling down all in their way, reached and surrounded the cart, whilst shouts of "Cheviot! Cheviot!" rent the heavens.

All was the wildest riot; but in that wild riot was Ruthven Somervil's safety. He and the priest vanished from the cart, and it seemed that the armed strangers mounted them both on steeds, and put swords in their hands.

And the victim was rent from between the very fangs of the destroyer! It was indeed so. All the power of Warkcliff could not bring that victim to the doom which the relentless knight had pronounced in his pride. He had flattered himself that he would cause that doom to be executed in the open face of day, and at his own market cross, that it might be a spectacle of his vengeance, and a terror to his foes. He had made a Gordian knot which he vainly imagined no one could or dared unloose—but the sword of the mosstrooper had severed it at a blow—and he must now fight to retrieve his stained honour, else that stain would disgrace him for ever.

The onset of the strangers had been so sudden and so fierce that it frightened the crowd and paralysed the armed guards. The great tumult and confusion admirably favoured the designs of the assailants. The scene became frightful; and not less so by the furious attack than by the shrieking of women, and cries of those unlucky wretches who were trampled down beneath the horses' hoofs. The horse which drew the condemned cart plunged from the hands of its driver, and rushed madly through the village. Roughly pressed upon, the gibbet quivered and shook like a tree in the storm, and at last fell with a crash. More died by the fall of that ghastly instrument of death than had died on it for many a year. Inextricable uproar and dismay reigned on every hand; for on every hand was the enemy.

De Ermstein's voice was heard at length exhorting his retainers to avert the disgrace which was falling upon them. The enemy were forcing a retreat down the village, carrying off the false priest and the condemned outlaw. Their object was retreat—retreat was their only safety, for they did not boast overwhelming numbers; fifty horsemen were perhaps their utmost force; but fifty horsemen only as they were, not a man amongst them but would have died ere Ruthven Somervil was re-taken. Down they galloped through the village amidst a tempest of shouts and the clash of steel.

And down like a torrent swept the forces of De Ermstein, headed by the old, stern-hearted knight, who would not relinquish his victim. His men seemed animated by his own fury, and, with a devotion worthy of a better cause, nobly seconded his efforts. The pursuit was hot. Away they swept in the wake of the mosstroopers. The village was cleared. They were careering through the valley, all in a confused and disorderly band. De Ermstein kept foremost, sometimes far in advance, for he rode with the fury of a blast. To take the outlaw, to drag him back to the fallen gibbet; he perilled his life—everything—to gratify his mortified pride and disappointed revenge. What disgrace it was to behold the outlaw free once more. Free! And on some following night the valley of Warkcliff might be gleaming with the red blaze of the burning village, and echoing the death-cries of the ravaged. The gibbet for the outlaw!

Amazed at the sudden rescue—snatched from death at the last moment—Ruthven Somervil's brain reeled and swam when he was dragged out of the condemned cart, and mounted upon a horse. It was so like a troubled dream. *Was* he rescued? He would have fallen from the saddle had not friendly and firm hands upheld him. He was sternly calm when the hangman approached him with the noosed rope in his hand—calm and collected *then*. But, when the first blow was struck, he became almost oblivious of what followed. And the great tumult that deafened his ear might have been the roaring of the tempestuous torrents of that unseen Jordan which rolls in darkness, washing the shores of Time and Eternity.

But, when the flight began, his recollection returned. He was in the midst of his men; he knew this one and the other around him in their disguises. Someone had put a steel cap upon his head, and he now found that he had a naked sword in his right hand, clutched as by the grasp of death. All at once he was restored to himself, saw and comprehended all clearly, felt his blood kindling in the headlong motion of flight, saw the pursuers following fast, brandished his sword, and faltered to his men, "Courage."

Courage? They had need of it. The pursuers were gaining upon them at every bound. The valley was far in the rear, hidden by the wreathing mists. The open Border was in front, and yonder stretched the blue heights of Cheviot. On and on; and now a scattered thicket received the mosstroopers. They were glad of its shelter, for the Southrons were at their heels.

"Halt! turn!" exclaimed Ruthven Somervil. "If we escape, we must bear these villains back. Turn upon them! Front De Ermstein! He will think of the disasters of Hawksglen and fly from our spears again."

At the stern word they halted, and reined round their panting steeds within the covert of the thicket, which prevented a general charge being made upon them. The Southrons, all scattered in twos and threes, came plunging up to the trees, as if in anticipation of an easy victory. But they had to fight the battle ere that victory could be won. The foremost daring spirits were received upon the hostile lances, and easily overthrown, some slain, others crushed beneath the weight or by the mad struggles of their transfixed horses.

Now came De Ermstein and the flower of his band. Their headlong assault was met by a straggling discharge of firearms, but the struggle came to be decided by the cold steel alone. Pressing upon each other, stumbling and trampling over their fallen comrades, the dying horses, and the thick bushes and underwood, they at last penetrated the thicket, and a deadly struggle, man to man, ensued. The outlaws were outnumbered; but who recked of a disparity of forces? They fought for their gallant captain's life—they fought and bled to humble the haughty pride and avenge the malice of the haughty and fierce-souled Sir Dacre. It was a confused, tumultuous conflict, for the combatants lost all union, and scattered themselves through the straggling wood, which was filled with battle and bloodshed and death.

The two foes, for whose sakes all this fatal strife was waged, eagerly sought the last mortal encounter. Ruthven Somervil was destitute of all defensive armour save the bascinet cap on his head; but, regardless of exposure, and with the irresistible fury of a lion, he threw himself into the thickest of the battle, bearing down, as with an arm of iron, all who dared to oppose him. His eagle eye glared through the thicket for the tall form of Sir Dacre, on whom he sought to wreak his vengeance. Hidden by the trees, or lost in the confusion, he could not now be seen. But at length he emerged into open view, and, ere either of them seemed aware, they met each other, knew each other at the first wild glance, and halted face to face.

"Miscreant!" gasped Sir Dacre, half-choked with fury. "The hangman's fell hand should have rid the earth of thee. Why should Fate throw thy worthless life upon the sword of an English noble?"

Somervil replied not to the insolence of his foe, but, brandishing his blood-dyed falchion, he spurred upon him. They encountered with a crash, and the outlaw's blade was shivered to the hilt. An instant's hesitation would have sealed his fate, but, almost flinging himself from his saddle, he grappled Sir Dacre's sword hand, and wrenched the sword from him. This was scarcely done when the plunging of their horses threw them both on the ground, locked in each other's arms, boiling with fury, gasping for breath. It was a death-struggle in all its fearful intensity.

Several of the outlaws, seeing their leader's danger, instantly abandoned their steeds and flew to extricate him and stab his adversary; but as many of the Southrons were equally ready to fly to the rescue of Sir Dacre, a mortal conflict ensued around the two struggling combatants. The false priest was conspicuous for his wild heroism, his trenchant blade, his voice of thunder; and the veterans of Hunterspath were there mingling in the strife to save their captain.

It seemed as though their aid was doomed to be unavailing, that they could not save the outlaw. His strength was unequal to that of the iron-nerved Sir Dacre, whose hand clutched his throat, whose knee rose upon his breast. Alas for the outlaw! A dagger glittered in Sir Dacre's grasp—glittered in the air—when a frightful voice arose above the din of battle, and arrested the clashing weapons, and a man, breathless, wounded, haggard, distracted in aspect, his eyes bloodshot and glaring, his head uncovered, his blood trickling to the ground—a spectacle of death and horror—staggered, with sinking strength, through the combatants, and seized Sir Dacre's uplifted hand.

"Mother of Heaven!" he gasped; "would you slay your son? Would you shed the blood of him whom you have lamented for twenty years?"

It was the gentle Johnston. At last the mighty secret was divulged. At last he had revealed, in the face of the world, the dark thought that so long wrung his heart and embittered his life. In the jaws of death, with his life-blood rushing from his wounds, he had avouched his guilt, and saved the father from a deed of unnatural guilt. By such a disclosure, at such a time, he had atoned for many of the crimes that lay heavy on his dark soul.

CHAPTER XIV.

"'Tis he! 'tis he himself! It is my son."

—*Douglas.*

WHAT a cry that was—"Would you slay your son?" Had the proud, noble, childless knight of Warkcliff—the last of his illustrious line—lamented the fate of the lost infant so long, and now was about to plunge his dagger into the breast of that very child? Had Heaven spared that child's life, and preserved him through many troubles, only that he might perish beneath the blow of the blinded father? The fateful, astounding words sounded to him like a death-knell; his hand relinquished the blood-stained steel, and he sprang from the ground, speechless and bewildered. As if by concert, the struggling parties forbore their fierce contest, and drew back with lowered weapons.

Exhausted and swooning in the struggle, Somervil, if he heard the startling exclamation, scarcely knew what it meant; his mind was wandering, his senses were failing him, his brain swam round, and, though relieved of the pressure of his adversary, he made no effort to rise from the earth, but lay supine, with scarce a movement of hand or foot.

Johnston, with his wild and haggard aspect, cast his bloodshot eyes around him; he staggered to and fro, and then fell prone on the turf.

"I only ask for breath—to disclose all this secret of woe," he gasped, as he turned on his side, and endeavoured to raise himself on his elbow—"breath to restore the lost son to the father—that is all I wish—and then let me die!"

What could the outlaws think of this? Their bold captain the son of their deadliest foe! They had striven with their blood and lives to restore him to the tower of Cheviot and to liberty, and it had resulted in the discovery that he was De Ermstein's son! Could they credit the incredible assertion from the mouth of a villain whose perfidy, falsehood, and guile they abhorred—whose very name they detested? No, no, it was but a fabrication of the dying ruffian. They would fight for their captain yet! Up with the slogan-cry and the deadly steel. Cheviot! Cheviot! Somervil should be borne off free.

With a wild shout they brandished their weapons; but their hostile attitude recalled the bewilderment of De Ermstein.

"Stay, stay," he shouted, almost in frenzy. "No more blood shall be shed. Implore all to stay the conflict. This secret must be disclosed. Somervil shall pass away free and scaithless though he be of no kindred to my house. Stay, stay!"

"Let us rest on the assurance of this noble knight," cried Reginald de Oswald. "His knightly word is passed for the safety of your leader. I for one will forbear further conflict," and he sheathed his sword.

His example was followed by such of the mosstroopers as were at hand, and, in a minute or two, the battle throughout the thickets had entirely ceased, and the combatants came all crowding together around the interesting group.

"Look to Somervil," groaned the gentle Johnston, pointing eagerly to the inanimate youth. "He may die of his wounds, and never look upon his father's face."

Comyn, Sinclair, and others of Somervil's band, instantly knelt around their captain. He was unwounded, but much bruised; his respiration was deep, his eyes were shut; but sensibility was returning, and he could answer, though faintly, when they spoke to him.

"Dacre de Ermstein," cried the gentle Johnston, "come hither to me. I have not many moments to live, but what remains of my mortal breath shall be devoted to the disclosure of this my blackest crime. Come hither."

De Ermstein rushed breathlessly towards him, bent over him, cast on his dark visage a look that might have pierced him through.

"I conjure you," he cried vehemently, "to disclose the naked truth, however deeply it may criminate you. I know you now—I remember your features, Johnston, and tremble to hear your revenge. Speak, speak, deceive not an agonised father. Restore to me my son, if your cruel hand spared my son to this mournful day."

"Ay," said Johnston, "my hand has long been cruel and dark with blood; but, cruel and ruthless as it is, it could not but spare the child o' De Ermstein. Behold your son—in Ruthven Somervil you behold him. And forgive me for the great wrong of the past in that I have saved you from the darkest crime that could stain living man!"

"My wife—his mother—pled sore for him," exclaimed Sir Dacre. "The mysterious sympathy betwixt mother and child had stirred her heart, and she would have saved him, though she was ignorant that he was the child of her youth and joy. And I spurned her prayer, and strove to incur a guilt which would have branded me with infamy, and crushed me with despair! My son! And can this be my son?" he faltered, as he thrust aside the eager crowd around the prostrate mosstrooper, and, throwing himself on his knees, threw his arms around the half-unconscious youth's neck, and gently raised his head to look upon him. It was a long, burning, searching gaze.

Ruthven opened his eyes.

"He has the look of his mother!" exclaimed Sir Dacre. "He has his mother's features! Why could I not remark this before?"

The little golden reliquary now attracted his eye, for it was half visible on the outlaw's breast, his doublet having been torn open in the struggle. In a moment Sir Dacre snatched it in his hand, and, in extreme agitation, he at length touched a secret spring in one of the edges, and the reliquary flew open, discovering within, in exquisite engraving, the Arms of Warkcliff, the name of *Stephen de Ermstein,* and the day and year of his birth,

"My son! my son indeed!" faltered Sir Dacre, letting the jewel fall back again upon the outlaw's breast. "But, as I remember, my child had a scar above his left temple—the scar of an accidental wound received in his infancy; that scar will close all proof," and, casting back the clustering hair from the outlaw's forehead, there was the scar, faint, indeed, but perceptible to the father's eyes.

This was enough. The proof was complete, even without the dying attestation of the gentle Johnston.

"My son! my long-lost son!" cried Sir Dacre, as, bursting into tears of joy, he folded the outlaw to his bosom. "The house of De Ermstein shall not yet be extinguished. Joy, joy! O, thou inscrutable Providence, how shall I offer my gratitude for this mighty boon?"

The mosstrooper heard the words of recognition—heard that he was called the son of De Ermstein, and heir of Warkcliff—felt himself pressed in the arms of a father. What were his emotions? The event was stupifying. And father and son rose from the ground with tumultuous feelings.

"You are safe—you will live?" cried Sir Dacre. "I have not stained my hands with your blood?"

The mosstrooper was unwounded. He might be giddy and faint; but not a life-drop of his had been lost. How the band stared in speechless amazement. No man could scarce credit what he heard and saw.

"Why did you not throw yourself into the arms of your father long ago?" cried Sir Dacre, in joyful reproach.

"Never till this moment," answered the outlaw, "did I know the secret of my birth."

"De Ermstein," groaned the dying Johnston.

"Ah, this man will reveal all," said Sir Dacre, and they all crowded around the jackman.

"I have restored the son to the father," said Johnston, with painful effort, for his life was ebbing away from him fast, "and I now can meet death, having, as I hope, expiated the darkest of my crimes. De Ermstein, here, with my last breath, I declare that youth your son. Cherish him and love him; he is of brave renown, and will bravely uphold the honour of Warkcliff. It is long since we parted, Sir Dacre, and I ha'e often wished ne'er to see your face again, for how could I look the man in the face whom I had wronged so basely?"

"It was by your hand, Johnston, that all my wrongs were inflicted," interrupted the outlaw. "Alas, what wrongs to expiate! but I forgive you."

"Had I not borne your father malice," answered Johnston, "you ne'er wad ha'e suffered what you ha'e suffered. But on my head, on my head alone, lies the whole weight of all your misfortunes. In my young days I was your father's jackman. In an evil hour, for some offence, he chained me in his Donjon, degraded me in the eyes of my comrades, and expelled me ignominiously from his service. My blood was hot, my brain was on fire, and I vowed revenge. I lingered about Warkcliff for some days, and one gloaming, being faint and weary, I lay down on a braeside, under the bield o' a bush, to rest my heavy head. Sir Dacre, you came riding by with your hunting train, and you set them upon me, and, in the desperate struggle for my life, I received a wound, the mark of which I shall bear with me to my grave. I was borne down by unequal numbers, and chased, like a wolf, before your hounds. Could I forgive that?"

"But your revenge was frightful," said Sir Dacre. "You might have spared the child; he was innocent."

"I knew that that child's life was dear to you," resumed Johnston. "Had I had the power, I might have come, with a ruthless band at my back, and filled all the valley of Warkcliff with smoke, and flame, and ruin; but *that* revenge would not have pierced you to the heart so deeply as I wished. No, Sir Dacre, I vowed a revenge which would crush you, and I had it, I had it! I came prowling back to Warkcliff, and watched my purpose like an adder coiled up to spring upon the victim. On the brae behind the castle I found your son in the nurse's arms—some of the other attendants had wandered to a little distance—and, unseen by any, I seized the infant from the woman's arms. She shrieked, and I struck her, and the blow cast her down the face of the brae. I then rushed away with the child." He paused for breath, and then continued his startling confession. "It was my intention to wring the child's life out, but my heart, rough as it was, revolted at a deed so felon and atrocious. I crossed the Border, and at last thought of a scheme by which I might also accomplish my revenge upon Elliot of Hawksglen. I once was in Elliot's train, but he, too, degraded me, and I detested him for it. In the dead of night I reached his castle. On the previous day I met with one of his retainers on the English Border, and accidentally learned the watchword at Hawksglen. This knowledge served me well, and bore me through the deep fraud. I knocked at the gate, answered the warder's interrogatory, and, when the gate was unbarred, I put the child in the old man's arms and fled. I flattered myself that I had sown the seeds of a deep revenge, for, thought I, should you discover that your son was in Elliot's power, you would charge upon him the crime of having bribed some miscreant to murder the nurse and seize the child."

"I would have charged him so," cried Sir Dacre, "had I known; for with Hawksglen I was ever at feud."

"Elliot protected the child," continued Johnston, "and brought him up as his own son—"

"And I was base enough," ejaculated Sir Dacre, "to levy war against the man who protected my son! Did he ever know the child's parentage?"

"Never," answered the outlaw captain; "but, after growing up to manhood, I was forced to abandon his house. In my helplessness I joined the band of Hunterspath; their leader was slain in a foray, and I was chosen in his stead."

"Did Elliot drive thee to desperation?" cried Sir Dacre. "Upon the villain's head I will visit it an hundred-fold."

"I have revealed all," said Johnston, who was fast sinking, "and now I can die in peace. It has long been a weary burden on my heart; but my heart is lightened of it at last. My dying moments are cheered by this restoration, even though it has come through crime and bloodshed. Embrace! Embrace!"

Father and son, so long apart, so wonderfully restored, fell, with an irresistible impulse, into each other's arms, and embraced with the intensest affection. The crowd of attendants burst out into a loud cheer, with which the wood resounded.

"But we shall hold merry times of it no more in old Hunterspath," said Ringan Sinclair, lugubriously, in the ear of Ellis Comyn. "Who would have thought our brave captain a Southron? And who shall be captain now?"

"Ah, but who can lead us to foray and fray," said Habbie Menmuir, "like Ruthven Somervil? To my mind, Ringan, our mosstrooping days are over."

"Often," said the gentle Johnston, "did my heart misgive me, and I yearned to restore the son to the father; but then the fierce and revengeful mood would come over me, and all my good thoughts were crushed."

"Had you come to Warkcliff," cried Sir Dacre, "and disclosed the secret to me, you would have been rewarded to the utmost. Why did your revenge last so long? The degradation of my son might have filled up your craving for vengeance, and led you to relent."

"I was present when your men took him," responded Johnston, "and I fought and shed my blood for him, and all was of no avail. Even his men detested me, and, when I offered to join them in a rescue, they scorned my aid. Wounded and feeble as I was, I set out to Warkcliff, and reached it on this morning, when I met with the band of Hunterspath, and heard from them the tidings that your son was to die. They had been informed by their spies of all that passed in the castle regarding his destined fate, and had come under disguise to attempt a rescue at the place of execution. I offered again to join them in the rescue; but they drove me away with detestation. They had no need of my aid, they said, for Ellis Comyn had entered the castle under the guise of a priest, and would save the captain. I again thought of throwing myself upon your mercy, Sir Dacre, and disclosing all; but terror overtook me, and I wandered up and down the valley like a madman. Then came the flight and the battle. I fought against you, and, at the last extremity, revealed the terrible secret."

His strength was almost wasted away, but still he struggled with death, for he still had something to crave of the outlaw. It was his forgiveness; and he freely gave it.

"One last request I have, which I implore you to grant," cried the dying man. "I will die here, but I fain would have my bones to lie beside those of my father and mother in the little kirkyard of Eburn, on the banks of the Teviot. I mind weel o' the day that I laid my mither's head in that grave; and I fain would rest beside her. When but a bairn I used to come in the gloamings wi' my mither, and sit doon aside the grassy hillock that rose over the remains of my father. The clods o' that kirkyard would be sweet to me."

Could the outlaw have rejected such a request, even to his worst foe? He granted it fervently. Johnston's head fell back; he was speechless, and his limbs were quivering in the struggle of death. But his parting moment was eased by the thought that he should sleep in the sod of that kirkyard which was endeared by the love of father and mother. Even his rude heart still retained some remnant of the old feelings and affections of childhood. He would lie in the grave of his kindred, with the water of Teviot murmuring sweetly past. There came a smile to his lips, and his eye flashed brightly for a moment like an expiring lamp. But the lamp of his life was quenched in the waves of Jordan. The gentle Johnston—that man of ruth and rapine—was no more!

And now De Ermstein and his son, with the greater part of their attendants, proceeded towards the castle. It should have been a progress of triumphal joy; but the joy was dashed with so much bloodshed. The strange tidings flew to the village before them, filling men's minds with amazement. The tumult in the village became greater than ever as the restored son approached, and those who had come out to see him die now surrounded him with shouts of welcome and demonstrations of gladness. And that gladness might have been greater had the stern knight listened to the solicitations of his lady, and not, with blind passion and with inflexible determination, hurried on a scene of tumult and death.

CHAPTER XV.

"Oh! princely is the Baron's hall,
    And bright his lady's bower,
And none may wed their eldest son
    Without a royal dower."

—*Wm. Kennedy.*

Who may imagine and depict the emotions of Lady de Ermstein on being presented with her long-lost son—that son whose loss was breaking her heart? Like one in a dream she heard the glad revelation, and beheld him with her eyes, and could even trace the features of the lost child; and, overpowered by the intensity of her feelings, she swooned away at his feet.

But the swoon was brief, and she awoke to happiness unalloyed. Throwing herself upon his breast, she wept in the fulness of her joy, and fervently gave thanks to Heaven for so eminent a blessing.

And from three hearts ascended bursts of gratitude to that over-ruling Providence, which, in omniscient wisdom, watches over and regulates human affairs. A blessing is intensified by the outpouring of a grateful soul. That very gratitude is a blessing in itself. Men whose minds are bound down and engrossed by the world may speak of this and that fortunate accident, and how well their efforts succeeded, and how skilfully they seized the all-important moment of Fortune; but a higher hand rules all things, and to that hand—the *cause*, and not the means—are all gifts to be assigned.

Thus had the outlaw discovered, at the eleventh hour, the secret of his birth. For years he had fondly cherished the conviction that he was descended from some noble line, and the whole effort of his life had been untiringly devoted to the discovery of his parentage. He had had his hours of deep depression and wild despair. As the clouds seemed to gather more thick and black around him, he often thought that they would never be dispelled; but always some hope cheered him on, and in that hope he was not deceived. And now there could be no obstacle to his union with the fair Eleanor; her hand he would instantly gain.

All the forenoon was spent by the parents and their son in the recital, by the latter, of the long and troubled history of his life. He detailed each incident; his love for Eleanor; his expulsion from Hawksglen; his union with the outlaws; his desperate adventures. The parents heard the singular narration with feelings of deep sorrow.

"I could fervently thank Elliot for having protected your infancy," said Sir Dacre; "but my gratitude is destroyed by his cruel expulsion of you at a time when your destiny might have become darker than it has been. It was a hardhearted, almost atrocious deed. Had he no thought that he would plunge you into despair?"

"It was not strictly an expulsion," answered the youth, "for I abandoned the castle to escape his reproaches and the insolence of his wife."

"That does not diminish his cruelty in my eyes," replied Sir Dacre. "What knight of honour and feeling would have so made unhappy and wretched the life of an orphan youth who had no other protector? Elliot has my gratitude for his care of your infancy; but my scorn and hatred for the unmanly violence which made you what you have been. And because you loved his daughter, too! It was a crime for the son of De Ermstein to love the daughter of a paltry Scottish chief!"

"But you should consider, husband, that Elliot had no knowledge of Stephen's birth," said the lady.

"No; he looked upon him as a beggar," rejoined De Ermstein. "Had he known my son's rank he would have strained every nerve, and employed every resource, fair or foul, to bring about an alliance which would ennoble his name. But he will eagerly seek such alliance now. Let him but hear this day's news, and I may have a daughter-in-law from Hawksglen to-morrow."

"I do not lay every blame upon Elliot's head," said Stephen, "for, had not his lady urged him on to hate me, I would never have left his house. He repents his errors, and would atone for them were it in his power. But, whatever his errors may be, let us never forget that he brought me up from infancy as if I had been his own. Thrown upon his mercy as a nameless, as an abandoned child, he cherished me with a bounty, a care, and an affection which have no bounds."

"You amply repaid all that bounty and care and affection," said the knight, "by defending him against inevitable downfall. Nevertheless, I will not mar our felicity by harbouring hatred against him. But I pray you to think no more of his daughter."

Stephen was prepared for this. But he was firm in his devotion to Eleanor; his heart never wavered from the fair object of its early choice. He told his father of that maiden's gentleness; that she had plighted her faith to him; that her love had known no change even in the depths of his degradation; that he would never forsake her; that he would make her his bride. Rather than that his vows should be slighted and broken, he would abandon the happiness which had come upon him.

The old knight's pride was wounded. There were many ladies in merry England, he said, of ancient name and high fortune, from amongst whom his son could choose a bride. But his son was inflexible. His mother joined him, and Sir Dacre's pride and wounded feelings at length gave way.

The castle was now filled with festivity, and a proud day it now was to him who had been so recently in the most dismal despair.

CHAPTER XVI.

"Fy, let us a' to the bridal,
For there'll be lilting there;
For Jock's to be married to Maggie,
The lass wi' the gowden hair."

—*Francis Sempill.*

NOTHING remains to close the tale save the nuptials of the hero and heroine. Everything has been briefly (and, we trust, satisfactorily) disposed of, so that, at the merry tinkle of the marriage bell, the curtain may fall, and nothing more be desired.

Stephen de Ermstein, in the ardour of his love, soon overcame all the objections which his proud-hearted father entertained to his proposed union with the daughter of Hawksglen. So soon as the necessary arrangements could be made, and the nuptial day fixed, Sir Dacre invited Elliot to spend some days with him at Warkcliff. Elliot went; and now these two, who had been enemies, buried their past feuds in oblivion. There were feasts and revels and hunting matches during Elliot's visit, and Warkcliff was full of rejoicing.

At length came the day on which Stephen was to lead his beautiful bride to the altar. It was a sunny day at the end of Spring. All was holiday and gladness in the village of Warkcliff. Floral arches spanned the resounding street, banners waved from the windows, and the porch of the old church was gaily decorated. Young and old were in their best attire, and on every face was joy.

Escorted by a numerous retinue of her friends, the bride had come to the castle that morning. Noon was the nuptial hour. The gladsome procession now left the castle amidst the thunder of guns from the battlement, the shouts of the people, and the loud strains of music. It was a gay and gaudy spectacle: the plumed horses, the foot-cloths of velvet that swept the ground, the blaze of gold and jewels, the floating banners, the armed men!

Never had Eleanor looked so beautiful, as now, with blushing cheeks and downcast eyes, she was led along to the altar to wed the youth of her heart's choice. The stormy time of sorrow was over, and the torch of love and hope burned purely bright.

In the brilliant sunshine the bridal party slowly approached the sacred fane, at whose altar two fond hearts were to be united for ever. Who could have foreseen this joyful hour when the young heir of Warkcliff had the cold world before him—a world without a friend?

And now the happy pair entered the church, and came before the altar and the priest. The blush of Eleanor grew deeper, and a tear of joy trembled in her downcast eye.

"Behold, while she before the altar stands,
    Hearing the holy priest who to her speaks,
And blesseth her, with his uplifted hands,
    How the red roses flush up in her cheeks."

The rite was soon concluded, and Eleanor was the blissful bride of Stephen de Ermstein!

THE END.

***

Printed in Dunstable, United Kingdom

72925026R00048